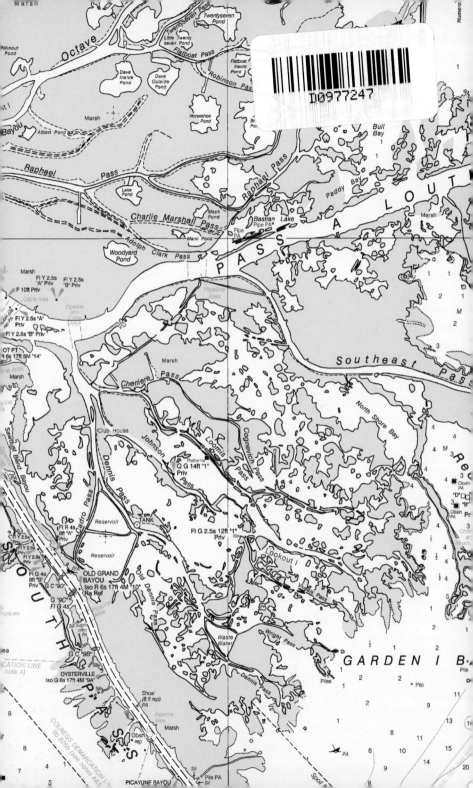

Copyboy

by Vince Vawter

CAPSTONE EDITIONS
a capstone imprint

Copyboy is published by Capstone Editions
1710 Roe Crest Drive
North Mankato, Minnesota 56003
www.mycapstone.com

Library of Congress Cataloging-in-Publication Data
Names: Vawter, Vince, author. | Trunfio, Alessia, illustrator.
Title: Copyboy / by Vince Vawter; illustrated by Alessia Trunfio.
Description: North Mankato, Minnesota : Capstone Editions,
[2018] | Sequel to: Paperboy. | Summary: Newspaper copyboy
Victor Vollmer sets out from Memphis to spread the ashes of
Mr. Spiro, his friend and mentor, at the mouth of the Mississippi
River, and with the help of new friend Philomene he may meet
the challenge.
Identifiers: LCCN 2018001840 | ISBN 9781630791056
(hardcover) | ISBN 9781684460205 (reflowable ebook)
| ISBN 9781684460199 (eBook PDF)
Subjects: | CYAC: Automobile travel—Fiction. | Interpersonal
relations—Fiction. | Stuttering—Fiction. | Newspaper
employees—Fiction. | Self-esteem—Fiction. | Family life—
Tennessee—Fiction. | Memphis (Tenn.)—History—20th
century—Fiction.
Classification: LCC PZ7.V4734 Co 2018 | DDC [Fic]—dc23
LC record available at https://lccn.loc.gov/2018001840

Designer: Kay Fraser

Cover illustration by Alessia Trunfio

End pages map by U.S. Department of Commerce/NOAA Office
of Coast Survey

Printed and bound in the United States of America.
899

To Nick Healy, a good editor
To Anna Olswanger, a good editor and agent
To Betty Vawter, a good editor and wife

Chapter 1

The obituary was the shortest one on the page that day. I clipped two copies—one for the newsroom library and one for my shirt pocket.

I punched out at the time clock, but instead of taking the elevator I walked down the five flights of stairs. I knew no one else would be taking the steps to the employee parking lot that early in the morning, and I didn't want to talk to anybody or even think about making eye contact.

I could feel myself about to lose it.

My copyboy job for the summer at *The Memphis Press-Scimitar* was going well, even though I found it repetitious. Clipping the newspaper. Filling paste pots. Changing typewriter ribbons. Tearing copy from the wire machines. I had to be at work at four every morning, but I didn't mind the work and I enjoyed the people.

Instead of putting the convertible top down on my car to let the stale overnight air escape, I slipped into the leather bucket seat, not wanting any reporters or copy editors just coming to work to see me.

I took the clipping out of my shirt pocket.

> **CONSTANTINE SPIRO, 79, a retired U.S. Merchant Marine, died Aug. 25, 1965, at Baptist Hospital after a brief illness.**
>
> **Mr. Spiro was born in New Orleans and moved to Memphis in 1955 after 40 years sailing the world's oceans.**
>
> **A spokesman for the Memphis Public Library said the deceased's small midtown house and extensive book collection have been donated to the library.**
>
> **No survivors listed. No services planned. M. J. Dodge Funeral Home has charge.**

I read the four paragraphs slowly and waited for the tears. They never came. My mind was already too busy trying to figure out how I was going to keep the special promise I made to Mr. Spiro before he died. The task ahead of me appeared simple enough, but I was beginning to learn that things weren't always as simple as they seemed.

★ ★ ★

My new way of dealing with my worries at home was to sit in my room and type words other people had written. At first I typed up anything that was handy, like stories out of the newspaper about the New York Yankees, but it came to me that I should type important words, ones that had been around for a while and meant more than what happened in a ball game.

I had been typing for most of the summer from a book Mr. Spiro had given me—*The Old Man and the Sea* by Ernest Hemingway. He gave it to me after I read in the newspaper about the writer killing himself with a shotgun. The short book ended up being my favorite, the way the old man was taken out to sea by the giant fish. I read it all the way through two times before I started typing it. The words felt perfect coming out of the ends of my fingers, almost as if leaving out a single one would cause the entire story to come crashing down—like the time my mother pulled a can from the middle of the stack at the grocery store and cans went everywhere.

Mr. Spiro would talk with me about the book anytime, and for as long as I wanted. How could someone write an entire book about catching a single fish, even if it was a gigantic fish? Mr. Spiro answered my question with a question of his own. He did that with me often. *What,* he asked, *if the book was about much more than just one man catching a fish?* That's when I read the book for the second time. Mr. Spiro could ask me a question like that, and it would be stuck in my head from then on.

My mother and father weren't going to be happy to hear about what I had promised Mr. Spiro on that last day I talked with him in the hospital. I needed to take my best shot at explaining to them how important it was for me to follow through on what I had told Mr. Spiro I would do for him.

Even though my stuttering was getting better when I had to talk to my parents, I still had trouble saying exactly what I wanted on account of my habit of substituting words to get to the starter sounds that came the easiest for me. I would begin to talk knowing exactly what I wanted to say, but then start substituting words to get to easier starter sounds. Before I realized it, the meaning of my sentences got tangled and tied up like double knots in my baseball cleats. A speech therapist that I once went to every week told me that changing and rearranging words all the time was taking the easy way out. She was right about it being a way out, but it wasn't all that easy. On the plus side, I learned to use a lot of new words that most people my age didn't know.

★ ★ ★

My parents sat at the supper table, not the one in the kitchen, but the big table in the dining room. My father had on his long-sleeve white shirt with cuff links and a tie, and my mother placed her silverware back where it was supposed to be even though we had finished eating. She always had to make sure the fork was on the left and the knife and spoon on the right with the sharp edge of the knife facing the plate. Those were her silverware rules when we ate in the dining room.

"I w-w-w- . . . need to tell you about a p----romise I made to Mr. Spiro." The *w* sound in "want" usually worked for me since it let out its own air, but all bets were off when I was nervous. I thought about changing "promise" to "vow," but I knew better than to try my luck on the *v* sound. I had to keep going as best I could.

"I t----old him I would spread his a----shes at the Mouth of the Mississippi River."

My parents looked at each other and back at me. I kept going, trying to remember to put a smooth pace to my words and to stick to exactly what I wanted to say, no matter how much the starter sounds threw me off.

"He said I should go down to N----ew Orleans and find the p----lace where the river becomes one with the sea."

I heard all Mr. Spiro's last words in my head and the grand way he used them, even though his heart was giving out toward the end and his voice was weak. I heard him say how he wanted me to offer up his ashes in four handfuls to match the four words on the corners of the dollar bill he gave me when I was his paperboy for a month one summer. His name for the four simple words was the "Quartering of the Soul." He told me that my spreading of his ashes would represent a final gesture in his attempt at a life well lived. I heard him call me "Messenger"— his name for me. I thought about telling my parents all his instructions so my parents could hear exactly what he said, but I didn't want his perfect words and the way he said them to be ruined by having them become all jumbled up in my mouth.

Not to my surprise, my mother was the first to weigh in.

"Absolutely and positively not."

She turned to my father and gave him her special look, the one that meant it was time for him to jump in and give her some backup.

"I really don't think it's a good idea, Victor. You really don't have that much time before you start college," he said.

I looked hard at my parents, first my father and then my mother. Even though we were eating at home, my mother was dressed up with her jewelry on like she was going out for the night. I looked straight into their eyes. Mr. Spiro taught me the importance of keeping eye contact. He said looking at a person and concentrating on their words might help me stop worrying so much about what was going on in the merry-go-round of words in my head. As good as Mr. Spiro was at talking, he was even better at listening and never taking his eyes off the person who was speaking.

My father folded his napkin by his plate and scooted his chair back from the table.

"You told me your coach wanted you to meet some of the guys before school started and throw a little with them. That would be a good way for you to get to know your new teammates."

At that point in the confrontation—and a doozy of a confrontation was exactly what I could feel it was shaping up to be—I decided to make the leap, to get everything I had on my mind out in the open. Mr. Spiro had an expression for it. In for a penny, in for a pound, he liked to say.

"N----ot sure I'm going to play b----aseball at Southwestern."

My bit of news shifted some of the attention away from the main subject on the table. My father didn't say anything, so my mother jumped in with both feet like she always managed to do.

"I can't believe you're saying that. You love to play baseball . . . and it's something that everybody agrees you're good at."

"Not as good as they think." It helped me to get a rhythm going with the *n* sound to start my sentences.

"I know you feel it might be time for you to start spreading your wings," my father said, "but you're just seventeen, and you don't need to be going all the way to New Orleans by yourself and certainly you shouldn't be taking on the Mississippi River by yourself, if that's what Mr. Spiro had in mind."

Another thing I was getting better at was waiting before opening my mouth. Mr. Spiro said silence was sometimes the best response during a verbal confrontation, seeing how it tended to keep the ball in the other person's court.

When I didn't say anything, my father had to keep going. "How would you even know where to find the Mouth of the Mississippi River?" he asked.

"It's about a hundred miles b----elow New Orleans." I had checked my encyclopedia before coming downstairs. The entry didn't give an exact location for the Mouth of the Mississippi River. I was looking for some kind of *X* on a map, but what it gave me was close enough for starters.

"For heaven's sake. That's in the middle of the Gulf of Mexico," my father said.

"No . . . not the middle." I didn't know exactly where the middle of the Gulf of Mexico was, but I knew it was more than a hundred miles from New Orleans.

"Well, maybe not precisely the middle, but you know what I mean, Victor."

The conversation had gone from my promise made to Mr. Spiro to my not playing baseball and then to the whereabouts of the mouth of the river. All the shifting around of the subject was good for my side since it's always harder to hit a moving target.

"Son, I know you liked your friend and I'm sorry he's gone, but I'm sure he didn't intend for you to go traipsing off by yourself to the Gulf of Mexico just to spread his remains."

"He d----id intend. Exactly what he intended."

"Well, I'm telling you what I intend," my mother said. "You are not going and that's that."

My mother was usually the one who laid down the law and told me I couldn't do stuff. That job fell to her since my father worked long hours and was out of town a lot. She had more practice than my father did in dealing with me, and she always had to keep piling it on after she had made her point with her famous "and that's that."

"So . . . you can just get all this river foolishness out of your head. You have better things to do than dumping somebody's ashes—"

"I DON'T HAVE BETTER THINGS TO DO!" My screams were never planned and always showed up without any kind of advance notice. I hated the way my voice sounded when I shouted and how it went completely out of control, with me turning red and sometimes slobber coming out of my mouth. The screams had started happening more frequently. On the bright side, I never stuttered when I screamed.

My mother flinched and rocked back in her chair. My scream had made the words bounce off the dining room walls, and I had slammed the palms of my hands on the table, which caused the supper dishes to rattle and my mother's silverware to jump out of place. The sharp edge of the knife ended up not even facing the plate anymore.

"Listen, young man, you will not talk to your mother like that," my father said, getting up from his chair. "Go to your room, and I mean right now."

It was hard for my father to raise his voice or sound mad, but he could do it if he had to when my mother was in the room and he needed to show her he was taking up for her.

I walked into the front entry hall and up the curved stairs. In our old house in midtown, which we moved away from six years ago, I could have gone straight up the back stairs to my room. I didn't like the house in the newer part of Memphis, even though my friends told me all the time how lucky I was to have a swimming pool and a good diving board with the extra spring in it.

My mother drove me batty talking about how much she liked the central-vacuum system in the new house. *Top-of-the-line,* she told all her friends when she showed it off. A tennis ball fit perfectly inside the wall where the hose was attached and would clog everything up so the vacuum wouldn't work. I tested it more than once, but I never had the guts to carry out my plan of vacuum cleaner destruction. That's the way it was with me. All plan, no action.

Chapter 2

Bedtime was early since my copyboy shift at the newspaper began at four o'clock in the morning, but I found myself at my typewriter anytime I was too upset to sleep.

My father knocked on my door. His knock was always two taps, much lighter than the way my mother banged before she opened the door and barged in.

"T----yping," I said through the closed door.

"I know, but I have an idea I want to run by you. May I come in?"

He didn't sound like he was going to yell at me any more. He could calm down from being mad quicker than anybody. I opened the door.

"I should have realized how important Mr. Spiro's last request was to you," he said. "I only met him that one time, but I liked him, too. I think I even talked to you about that."

I was at Mr. Spiro's house on a Saturday afternoon when a rainstorm stranded me there on my bike. My father happened to be in town that day and came to pick me up. Mr. Spiro invited him into his small house, with all the wooden crates filled with books he had gathered from his Merchant Marine travels around the world. Mr. Spiro made coffee and the two of them talked for a long time considering they didn't have much in common. I liked seeing them together. And especially hearing them. Mr. Spiro spoke to my father in the same out-of-the-ordinary way he talked to me, using his grand words that made everything he said special. He never changed how he talked no matter what the subject or who was listening.

My father sat down on one of my twin beds.

"It's nice that Mr. Spiro had the confidence in you to ask this favor, but we need to look at what some of our options might be."

I wasn't sure of the proper word for what Mr. Spiro asked me to do, but "favor" was not the right word in my book.

"Did Mr. Spiro say exactly when he thought the ashes might need to be delivered—or disbursed—or whatever the proper term is?"

"N----ot exactly."

I could outlast my father on eye contact. He glanced around my room at the bookshelves along the walls. My mother had been saying that she wanted to buy bookcases to replace the shelves I had put together from bricks and unfinished planks of wood the workers left behind after they built our house. She had not gotten around to buying the bookcases yet, and I hoped she never would. I liked how I could change the height of the shelves by just adding or taking away bricks, and how I could put my hands on any book without a lot of fuss.

"Here's what I think might be a good option. See what you think about this." My father's all-business voice told me he had spent a good amount of time coming up with his idea. "You know that business takes me to New Orleans occasionally. You and I could take the plane down on my next trip and we could see about going out on the river or possibly even the gulf. How does that appeal to you?"

His offer surprised me, especially the way that he seemed to be even a little excited about the idea. My father always said the thing he liked most about the work at his accounting firm was "putting deals together to the satisfaction of all parties involved." His offer sounded to me like one of those put-together deals.

"Wh----en would we go?"

"I don't have anything down there in the next few months, so it would probably have to be sometime next spring, but surely before the start of heavy tax season."

What did "tax season" have to do with anything? I wasn't even sure when tax season was or why it had to be called a season. "That m----ay be too far off," I said.

My father hesitated before he spoke. He was more careful than my mother with his words when he answered me. "Your promise was a gesture on your part to honor your friend. It seems to me there shouldn't be a deadline attached. You can think about it. We have some time."

My father looked at my bookshelves again.

"You're getting quite a collection of books, aren't you?"

He was setting me up for a change-up pitch with some beating around the bush and small talk.

"Now, what's this about not wanting to play baseball at Southwestern?"

Exactly the change-up pitch I was expecting.

"C----an we talk about it another time? N----eed to think about it some more and I have to be at work early in the morning." I yawned and it wasn't one of my fake yawns I could pull off when I didn't want to talk to somebody. I had been up since three o'clock that morning.

"Okay, but I'd like to have a conversation about it before you make your decision. Playing ball is a good way for you to make new friends and feel comfortable in new surroundings." He stood and started for the door. "Oh, your mother said to remind you that we're having company for dinner tomorrow night. Just a client or two and their wives. There'll be plenty in the refrigerator for you anytime you get hungry."

When my parents didn't invite me to eat with them and their friends, I was relieved, but I also wondered sometimes if they were trying to keep people from hearing the way I talked. Their friends asked me questions that made word substitution impossible, like *What grade are you in?* or *Where do you go to school?* They never thought to ask questions like *Who is your favorite baseball player?* I had a choice of a dozen good answers for a question like that since the answer really didn't matter and I could choose whatever starter sound felt good at the time.

Even if I was on the opposite side of the conversation, I was always in a better mood after talking with my father than after talking with my mother. That confused me, seeing as how I had found out years before that although I had my father's name, I didn't have anything else that belonged to him. Some other man was my blood father and was responsible for making me with my mother. I didn't have a clue who it was or why it happened. I just knew it to be a fact after I found some official papers in a closet I wasn't supposed to know about.

Thinking about that discovery always started me pounding on my typewriter.

* * *

Before the company came the next day, there would be time to eavesdrop on my parents to find out what they were thinking and saying about me and the promise I had made to Mr. Spiro. It was much easier to listen in on them in our old house with the way the sound carried up the back stairs, which were bare wood that seemed to amplify the sounds from below. Our new house was crazy with carpet, even on the stairs, making it harder to listen in on conversations I wasn't supposed to hear. I wasn't proud of all the snooping around and eavesdropping I had to do to find out what was going on in my own life, but the way I saw things with my parents, it was two against one and so I thought it was okay to cheat a little. When I told Mr. Spiro I had listened in on my parents, he scolded me in his gentle way: "If you must eavesdrop, make sure it is on your own thoughts." I was having trouble sticking to his suggestion.

Mam also used to get upset with me for listening in on my parents.

Mam lived over the garage in the back of our old house in midtown and cooked for us and practically raised me, but she went back to Coldwater, Mississippi, when we moved into our new house.

I missed Mam as much as I knew I was going to miss

Mr. Spiro. The two people I liked to talk to the most and now both were gone out of my life.

I needed to get to sleep but wanted to type a few more paragraphs before turning off my desk lamp. The story was getting to the good part where the old man in his small boat way out in the Gulf of Mexico was about to hook the giant fish.

Reading the words could take me out of my room and into the Gulf Stream, but typing the words was even better. I could hit the keys harder when the old man needed help fighting the sharks that came to steal his big fish.

Chapter 3

At five o'clock in the morning the editors who put together the first edition of the *Press-Scimitar* began to arrive in the newsroom. Although the newspaper was called an "afternoon," the one-star edition had to be on the street by eleven o'clock so the lunch crowd would have some news to read.

Charles Roker was the first editor to come in on the copydesk each morning. He edited and wrote headlines for the overnight stories he picked out for the newspaper from the reams of wire copy I tore off the Teletype machines. He'd taught me to separate the copy in a certain way, matching stories on the same subject from all the different news services to which the newspaper subscribed. Pairing up the wire stories was the only part of my copyboy job that took any real brains. I liked reading the stories coming in from all over the world and seeing how reporters told about the same event in different ways.

Since Mr. Roker had to dive in to his work as soon as he took his seat, I usually went down to get his first cup of coffee in the newspaper's lunchroom, the "ptomaine tavern" as he liked to call it. He usually gave me a small tip, saying, "To the Victor go the spoils." In a way Mr. Roker reminded me of a younger and funnier version of Mr. Spiro. He could joke and be serious at the same time, and packed a lot of expression into the words he used and stories he told.

"How's our chief copyboy and bottle-washer today?"

"Wire machines are spewing out a lot of c----opy this morning."

"That's not good," Mr. Roker said. "I think I closed down the Poor & Hungry last night at the shuffleboard table, and it must have slipped my mind to go home. Sleep is highly overrated, don't you think, Vic?"

He winked at me. That summer I had seen him, several times, coming out of the shower on the first floor that the pressmen used to wash off the ink after their shifts. I took it he had come straight to the newspaper from having a night of fun with his friends.

"I'll get your c----offee . . . and c----ould I talk with you if you have time when I get back?"

"You bet. It might even slow you down from bringing me so much copy." He pointed to three big stacks I had put in front of him. "You do make it easier, I'll have to say. You're the only one of our copyboys who knows his butt from Bombay and has sense enough to pair up stories correctly."

I was a paperboy for a month when I was eleven years old—the summer I met Mr. Spiro—but this was delivering the news in a new way.

"It's sort of fun."

Mr. Roker laughed. "Your idea of fun is nothing like mine."

Mr. Roker and the other copy editors worked on a horseshoe-shaped desk called "the rim." The chief of the copydesk sat in "the slot" next to a pneumatic tube that snaked up to the ceiling and then curved down to the composing room on the floor below. Every word and picture in the newspaper came through the editors on the copydesk. It was like an assembly line of stories, headlines, and photographs.

Mr. Roker had worked at several newspapers around the South. I liked to hear him tell his stories in his special way. I overheard him once holding forth on the subject of New Orleans jazz. He played the saxophone and talked a lot about the music of New Orleans that he liked so much.

I rushed back with his steaming mug of black coffee.

"Can you stand up a spoon in it?"

"M----aybe."

"Excellent. My stomach needs a good coating of that road tar this morning."

He took a long and careful sip.

"Tastes like excellent paving material. Now, what can I do for the Victor this morning?"

My routine copyboy duties gave me a lot of time to think about how I was going to ask my questions. I had them in my head, but that didn't mean they were going to come out of my mouth the way I had planned them.

"D----o you know . . . ?" I started my question on a bad sound. I wanted to get it exactly right, so I backed up and took another run at it. "Can you tell me the best way to get to N----ew Orleans . . . from here?"

"Take Highway 51 South, and stop just before you hit the Gulf of Mexico." Mr. Roker continued to read wire copy, setting some aside and sticking the rest on a long metal spike.

"The G----ulf of Mexico is actually where I'm going."

Mr. Roker looked at me.

"Are you planning on hopping a freighter or something?"

My answer needed to sound like the casual chatter of the newsroom, the type of conversation I was lousy at.

"C----ould be. Maybe. The place I really have to get to is the Mouth of the Mississippi River, which is somewhere in the Gulf of Mexico."

"I'm afraid my New Orleans expertise ends at a certain bar in the French Quarter on Toulouse Street."

"D----o you know anyone who might help me find my way around if I could g----et myself to New Orleans?" My question sounded bold. I wasn't sure it was the kind of question you asked someone you had known for less than three months and who was many years older.

"You seem to be a might serious about this trip."

"I am . . . serious, serious." My double-word trick I used sometimes sounded strange and wasn't good grammar, but it got my point across.

"Well then, my serious answer in return is that I know someone who probably knows someone who could accommodate you if he can't."

"C----an you tell me about him?"

"I have a good friend at the *Times-Picayune* who always has a good answer even when there's not a good question handy. If you'd like, I could let him know you're coming." Mr. Roker picked up the black pencil he used to edit copy for the composing room. "Remind me again, Vic, of your last name."

I put my top teeth on my bottom lip to make the starter sound I hated so much—the *v* sound. I would have to take several gulps of air and draw out the sound to make sure it came out, but my last name—Vollmer—would make it out of my mouth eventually. One way or another.

★ ★ ★

After my four-hour shift, I drove to a spot downtown on the cobblestone banks of the Mississippi River to read the obituary again. The sense of a plan coming together had replaced the empty feeling of Mr. Spiro being gone. The afternoons and weekends I spent talking with him about books and the places he had been during his time at sea felt more important to me than the years I spent at school.

I read the four paragraphs under my breath and put the clipping back in my billfold next to Mr. Spiro's taped-together dollar bill that I looked at every day.

When I was Mr. Spiro's paperboy for a month six years ago, he gave me a weekly paperboy tip that wasn't actual money. It was much more than that. Each Friday he presented to me a corner of a dollar bill with a single word written on it. Each word started with the letter *s*. Anytime I asked about the four words— student, servant, seller, seeker—that made up the dollar bill, Mr. Spiro would say only that the words represented the Quartering of the Soul, and that I would come to understand how they fit together if I continued to think about them.

My promise to take Mr. Spiro where he wanted to go seemed a way for me to work out once and for all exactly how the four words were connected. I had an idea what they had to do with one another, but some time alone in my car would help put the finishing touches on my thoughts.

It was just like my father to come up with a plan to take me to New Orleans, but the trip to the Mouth of the Mississippi River couldn't wait on something like tax season. My job at the newspaper that I liked so much would be ending soon and then college would start and I didn't know how that was going to go. I needed to take Mr. Spiro to his place at the end of the river as soon as possible. At least I would have that part of my life figured out.

I stepped out of my car onto the slick cobblestones on the riverbank and picked up a stick of driftwood. I heaved it as far out as I could into the fast-moving current of the wide river. Mr. Spiro once explained to me that a drop of rainwater falling in Memphis would travel the four hundred miles to New Orleans in ten days. I figured it would be about the same for a piece of driftwood, give or take a day or so. Somehow, I was going to beat that piece of wood to New Orleans and then on to the Mouth of the Mississippi River.

Chapter 4

Two taps on my bedroom door.

"I hope you're not asleep. Our company stayed a little longer than we expected," my father said.

He walked in with his pad of green paper he liked to make notes on when he talked business with his clients.

"I received an unusual call at the office today from a lady at the main library." The top page of the pad was filled with my father's handwriting. "I think she was actually trying to get in touch with you but I went ahead and talked with her."

"What about?"

"Were you aware that Mr. Spiro owned some valuable first editions and other rare books?"

"He had a lot of b----ooks, but I didn't know about them being v----aluable."

"The lady I talked to said the library's conservator estimated the value of the collection to be more than twenty-five thousand dollars." My father was good at saying and using large numbers. I had to add the zeros in my head.

I put down the volume of the encyclopedia I was reading, which had a long section about the Mississippi River. My father took out the mechanical pencil he always kept in his shirt pocket and made a check mark on the pad.

"Let's see here. One of the books was published in 1896, and was a first edition of an English translation about somebody named Zara-thus-tra." He spelled the name. "The lady said just that one book alone in its leather binding could be worth as much as five hundred dollars."

I nodded. "That was written by a guy named N----ietzsche. *Thus Spake Zarathustra*. It's a book about a man who lived in a cave somewhere and spent his days thinking about important stuff."

My father nodded and smiled like he understood what I was trying to explain to him. He made another check mark on his pad.

"There were some other first editions, mostly in French, that she said were worth more than a hundred dollars each. Conservatively."

I saw in my head the wooden crates of books that were stacked on one another and covered the walls of Mr. Spiro's small house, which I visited many times.

"The woman at the library said that my name—I guess it was actually your name—was the only one found in the house and she wondered if we would be making any claims against the estate."

"What kind of c----laims? What did you tell her?"

"I told her 'no,' obviously."

"G----ood. I didn't know any of Mr. Spiro's books were v----aluable in a money sense, but I remember him telling me that he wanted everything to go to the library when he . . ." I could say the word to finish the sentence, but I didn't want to hear it, so I let it go.

I wanted to tell my father about the conversation that Mr. Spiro and I had one afternoon where he explained that a person never really owned things like books and paintings or even houses. We just borrowed those things while we were here on the Earth. A person could only own something, Mr. Spiro said, if that something couldn't be touched or held. Things like the knowledge that comes out of books and friendship and good memories.

But I didn't know how to talk to my father about things like that, so we just looked at each other.

"Have you thought any more about us flying down to New Orleans in the spring?" he asked.

My plans were going in another direction. Lying to my mother didn't bother me much, but lying to my father always left me sad. But I could do it if I had to.

"Still thinking," I said.

"We could make a nice family vacation out of it. Your mother could do some spring shopping in New Orleans and maybe if we did go out in the gulf, we could try to get in a little deep-sea fishing. Kill two birds with one stone, so to speak."

Deep-sea fishing? Why couldn't I make my parents understand that keeping my promise to Mr. Spiro shouldn't have anything to do with a family vacation or killing two birds with one stone?

When something upset me down deep, my stomach started acting like it did during those complete speech blocks I had when I was younger. The sour taste of bile worked its way up in my throat and into my mouth. I had two ways to go. I could let loose my out-of-control scream or I could drop myself into a kind of trance. I had never screamed at my father. I had to swallow to push the bitter taste back down out of my mouth.

My father was good at recognizing my hypnotized look when I went into a trance. He patted my foot.

"Well, I know I would enjoy the trip," he said. "Let me know when you want to talk about it some more."

He walked out of my room and closed the door.

It was too late at night to start typing. The only way to replace my feeling of being alone was to think about how I was going to honor my promise to Mr. Spiro. The idea of taking him to the mouth of the river on my own kept him alive in my head. I know that's why the tears never came.

★ ★ ★

The newspaper's managing editor, the man who hired me for the summer, had put a note on the paste pot at my worktable telling me to be sure to come to his office before I left work for the day. He didn't come to work until nine o'clock, so that meant there was an extra hour for me to get nervous over what he might want to talk with me about.

Even though off the clock, I checked all the typewriters in the newsroom to see if any needed new ribbons. Tending to the typewriters was one of my copyboy duties I enjoyed most. A cotton swab soaked in pure alcohol I brought from home was my trick for cleaning out the ink and the residue from the carbon paper that gunked up the key hammers. The typewriters were a mess until I started working on them. One reporter even thought someone had switched typewriters on him since the letters looked so different after I cleaned his keys.

The managing editor motioned through the glass walls of his office for me to come in.

"My sense is that you enjoy working here," he said. "Is that right, Vic?" I nodded. "Aren't you starting school at Southwestern this fall?"

"Y----es, sir. This is my l----ast week working here."

"That's what I want to talk to you about. What would you think about continuing to work part-time during school?" He let his question hang in the air. "I know Southwestern is a demanding place and you'll want to keep your grades up so you can stay out of the Vietnam draft, but the copydesk chief says you've been doing a good job. This would let you keep your hand in, so to speak."

The managing editor always looked down at the newspaper when he was talking to someone. He had a lot to learn about good eye contact.

"W----ould I be doing the same job?"

"Oh, we might have you start doing things like typing in the dog-track results and the cotton futures. The copydesk tells me you're pretty good on a typewriter."

"I'd like that, but c----an I think about it?"

"Sure, but let me know soon so we can get you on the work schedule."

The phrases "doing a good job" and "good on the typewriter" rested comfortably in my head as I walked out of his office and into the busy newsroom. My high school baseball coach often said "good job" after I pitched a no-hit inning, but this was a real job, more than a game. With Mr. Spiro gone, the thought of also having to say goodbye to the people I had gotten to know at the newspaper was starting to bother me.

Even abandoning the newsroom typewriters wasn't sitting well with me. I was eight years old when I started banging on a typewriter that had come from my father's office. I typed with one finger at first and at some point moved on to two fingers. In my sophomore year I applied to take a typing class that was only for juniors and seniors. To get the waiver to take the class, I had to stand up and give a speech in front of the assistant principal and the typing teacher on why I was requesting the exception to the rule. I practiced what I was going to say for two weeks. I gave my speech with the sweat pouring off me and my starter sounds resembling noises made by zoo animals, but somehow I got through it and they let me take the class early. Typing meant that much to me.

Out in the newsroom, everyone's pace was picking up with the deadline closing for the first edition.

Reporters worked the telephones for the second edition and updated their stories from the previous day. Galley proofs several feet in length came up in pneumatic tubes from the composing room. Police scanners and a shortwave radio crackled at the city desk. Photographers slapped up dripping black-and-white photographs to dry on a sheet of heated metal. The chemicals in the photos gave the room an odor like a starched shirt that had been singed with an iron.

My early shift didn't let me see this scurry of activity in the newsroom.

"N----eed another cup of coffee, Mr. Roker?"

"What are you still doing here?" he asked. "And for the love of saints, stop calling me 'Mr. Roker.' That was my father's name. Charlie is my name."

I cleaned the old wire copy off the copydesk spikes and took a pile of grainy wire photos to the library for filing. Most people at the newspaper referred to the library as the "morgue." Not me. I made a note to change the print-blade on the wire-photo machine on my next shift and then went to the third-floor lunchroom for coffee.

"Here's your r----oad tar, Charlie." I handed him the steaming mug.

"You still want me to call my friend in New Orleans?"

"Yes, if I can g----et some things worked out, I'm g----oing down there early next week."

"Man, if I wasn't completely out of vacation, I'd go with you. You ever been to New Orleans?"

"Only with my parents."

"Let me assuage you, my son. New Orleans is best experienced without parents anywhere near."

"Assuage" was a word that didn't come up often in normal conversation, but I liked words like that. You could hear anything in the newsroom if you kept your ears open. Once when the copydesk chief saw me refilling paste pots, he told me I performed my duties with "élan, aplomb, and éclat." He was kidding with me, but his words sent me running to the dictionary. The copydesk chief worked the crossword puzzle in the paper each day with an ink pen. Most of the time he finished it without having to cross out any words.

Above the copydesk, the ceiling was full of pennies stuck in the acoustic tiles. Hundreds of pennies. The custom among the copy editors was to fling a penny at the twenty-foot ceiling anytime the copydesk chief handed out an "atta-boy" for a headline he judged to be especially well written. You got only one shot at making the penny stick in the ceiling, a sign of good luck.

The newspaper plant had once been a place where automobiles were manufactured. When the two-story tall printing presses cranked up, the building shook and a penny or two might drop from the ceiling. The copy editors would start singing "Pennies from Heaven." That always cracked me up.

I was tempted to try the penny toss in the early mornings when no one was around to see, but I figured the game was off limits to me in my lowly status as a copyboy.

The idea of my summer job turning permanent excited me, even though working and going to school at the same time would be difficult. There weren't many places where I felt comfortable. Like I belonged. The newsroom was different. The typewriters. The people. The words.

I already was sure that keeping my job at the newspaper was what I wanted, but I had to figure out how it could work out with my plans to find the Mouth of the Mississippi River. I needed time off. I was set on keeping my promise to Mr. Spiro with élan, aplomb, and éclat.

Chapter 5

The M. J. Dodge Funeral Home was a single-story building of white brick with black canvas canopies over doorways on three sides. The building looked as if it had been added on to several times, which made it difficult to decide which door was the main entrance. My mother would have told her friends that the building was *not in the best part of town,* but everything looked clean and well kept to me.

The ad in the Yellow Pages said the funeral home opened for business at eight-thirty. I had come straight from work. The only car in the parking lot besides a white hearse and two black limousines was an older Ford Fairlane.

I chose the entrance with the longest canopy. The lights inside the main hall were dim and the floor was covered with a thick carpet that showed footprints. One room off the hall had lights on and the door was open. A woman about the age of my mother smoked a cigarette and turned pages of the morning newspaper at her desk.

I stood in the doorway until she looked up at me.

"Can I help you?"

"Is this where I p----ick up ashes for a friend?"

The woman took off her eyeglasses that were attached to a small chain around her neck.

"I assume you're talking about crematory remains. And did you say you're picking up the remains *for* a friend?"

"My f----riend is the a----shes."

Even if you took away the stuttering, my sentences sounded ridiculous. None of the words sounded right.

"A licensed mortician will need to release any remains." The woman adjusted the chain and her glasses.

"Mr. Spiro t----old me I'm the only one who is supposed to p----ick him up. He t----old me so himself." The more words that came out of my mouth, the sillier they sounded.

"I'm not sure I understand you. Can you tell me the deceased's name? I'll see if we have a file."

I thought about pulling the newspaper obituary out of my billfold and showing it to the woman, but Mr. Spiro never wanted me to cheat like that by showing words on paper. I could see his name stamped in block letters on his old duffel bag he carried all over the world. I had never said his first name out loud. I could feel the hard *c* sound that started the name looming ahead of me. I didn't want to stutter on it, so I whispered "It's" for a soft starter sound and then shouted "CONSTANTINE Spiro."

The woman slid her chair back from her desk. She glared at me.

"I'm not deaf, you know. What's the date of death?"

Saying words when I didn't have any options like names and dates always put extra pressure on my stuttering.

"Au----gust twenty-fifth, n----ineteen sixty-five."

The woman made a big deal of taking off her glasses again and giving me a hard stare like she wanted to be sure to let me know she thought I was in way over my head.

"Yes, young man. I assumed it to be the current year."

It was getting tough for me to hold it together in the funeral home, the first one I had ever been in by myself.

"Let me go check in the back. About the remains. Take a seat." She said the words in a way that let me know she thought I was bothering her.

The word throwing me off the most in the funeral home was "remains." Ashes were not all that "remained" of Mr. Spiro. Everything "remained." In my head. Especially our long conversations on Mr. Spiro's front porch or surrounded in his house by his crates of books, and maps of the world hanging on the walls. Also the fact "remained" that Mr. Spiro had a lot to do with my speech getting better even though I was having one of my off days at the funeral home. Mr. Spiro was the one person I could talk with about my stuttering after I convinced my parents I should stop going to my speech therapist and try more to work things out on my own. Mr. Spiro always said instead of me trying to stop stuttering, I should only think about finding my voice, a voice that may or may not include stuttering.

I heard the funeral-home woman talking to someone in the back room. A man in a black suit and hair that was combed straight back came into the room carrying a manila folder.

"Are you Mr. Victor Vollmer the Third?"

"Y----es, sir."

"We were expecting someone older, but, be that as it may, let's step next door to my office and see what we have."

The funeral home manager made a big deal of spreading out the contents of the folder on his desk.

"We have some paperwork to do, but it won't take long since the account has been prepaid," he said. "First, I'll need to see some identification."

The manager took my driver's license, studied it, and scribbled on a pad.

"We seem to have a problem here, Mr. Vollmer. I can't release crematory remains to a minor."

"B----ut I'll be eighteen soon."

"I can do the math, Mr. Vollmer. State law states specifically that bodily remains cannot be released to anyone not yet twenty-one years of age."

"B----ut it was Mr. Spiro who said that I should p----ick him up."

The funeral home manager was as good as I was at strong eye contact. He probably had a lot of chances to practice in the business he was in. He also was good at calling me "Mr. Vollmer" in a certain way meant to let me know he didn't consider me a real "Mr." yet. We stared each other down.

"You'll need to bring your father or mother in with you to act as a signatory."

"C----an't do that."

"And may I ask why not?" He was getting snooty like the woman in the first office.

"Well, my p----arents aren't . . . they're out of town."

The manager made a big deal of closing the folder.

"Then we'll just have to wait for them. We don't violate

state law at M. J. Dodge, so your parents or an appropriate legal guardian will need to come in at some point and sign for the crematory remains before I can release them."

* * *

Sitting inside my car in the parking lot, I pounded the steering wheel. My visit to the funeral home was a complete failure, but I was more upset at myself. I had walked out of the building so confused and upset that my first thought was that I should drive to Mr. Spiro's to ask him what to do next. Like he was still alive. Like the old man in the boat who kept talking out of his head to the boy who wasn't there.

Taking possession of Mr. Spiro's ashes was the first hurdle of my trip and I had not done well. You don't have to be by yourself in a small boat in the middle of the ocean to feel alone.

* * *

Typing from the book up in my room helped to calm me after I got home. I was getting to the part where the old man tried to fight off the sharks with a knife tied to one of his oars. That part of the story always made me hit the typewriter keys hard like I was jabbing at the sharks the way the old man did in the book. Sometimes I would even find myself looking around my desk to make sure sharks weren't circling me.

Banging on my typewriter wasn't going to get me any closer to the Mouth of the Mississippi River, but I didn't know what else to do. The old man said that a person could be destroyed but not defeated. I was not going to be defeated. I typed most of the afternoon and into the night.

* * *

The dented Ford Falcon pulled into a parking space next to me at the funeral home the following afternoon. Charlie Roker climbed out. Instead of a short-sleeved shirt and tie like he usually wore at the newspaper, he had changed into a nice business suit like my father wore most of the time.

"I put these monkey clothes on in August only for people I truly admire," Charlie said. "Count yourself in an ultra-exclusive club with very few members."

"Thanks for h----elping me. I'll be h----appy to buy you gas or—"

"Hush. Let's get this show on the road so I can get out of this worsted-wool straightjacket."

I had explained to Charlie at the newspaper that morning about the promise I had made and what I was up against at the funeral home. He asked me a bunch of questions, and I ended up telling him about Mr. Spiro, everything from his days as a Merchant Marine to the little house filled with books. I even told the story about the time I first met Mr. Spiro when I was his paperboy and I passed out on his porch trying to say my name. I showed Charlie the taped-together dollar bill with the four words, and we talked about what the Quartering of the Soul might mean. Charlie said he wished he could have known Mr. Spiro for the simple reason that the world didn't have enough people in it like him.

I peeked in the door of the funeral home manager's office.

"H----ere's my legal guardian." My words came out rehearsed and my voice was too loud, something that happened anytime my nerves got the best of me.

Charlie stepped into the office and stuck out his hand.

"Charles Roker, sir. Nice to meet you."

"And you are the legal guardian of young Mr. Vollmer here?"

"You are correct, sir," Charlie said. "I'm his uncle on his mother's side. His parents travel extensively and when they're out of town I assume full legal guardianship."

The manager stared at us like he was trying to think up another question, but Charlie didn't give him an opening.

"You should be aware that my nephew and I were best of friends with Constantine Spiro. We have special services planned down in New Orleans for our late companion," Charlie said. "I think it's great that Constantine asked Vic here to be in charge of the transportation."

"I was just about to ask what considerations you might have for the remains since I need to make a note in our records for the state." The manager made his voice sound more official when he spoke to Charlie.

Charlie shot me a quick look and zeroed back in on the manager.

"Certainly. As you must know, our Constantine Spiro was a man of the sea . . . and, as such, we are going to give him a proper burial. We have an appropriate ceremony planned in the New Orleans harbor with other friends and acquaintances. The Coast Guard will take part. Cannons will roar and good friends will salute as our sailor and his ashes are returned to the sea."

Although his breath didn't smell like it, I wondered by the way his eyes twinkled if Charlie might have had a beer or two on his way over to the funeral home. The manager appeared to be impressed with what Charlie was saying, which was all that mattered.

"Very good," the manager said. "We just have a few

documents to complete and notarize and you can be on your way."

The manager called in the snooty woman from the office next door to be a notary. Charlie signed his name so no one could possibly make it out. The woman left the room without looking at me.

"You know, it's odd that the deceased listed no family or relatives when he made his arrangements with us," the manager said. "It seems like a man of his stature—"

I interrupted. "Mr. Spiro d----idn't have time for . . . for such or----dinary stuff . . . or for . . . whatever things other people like." I realized as soon as I opened my mouth that it wasn't a good idea for me to attempt to join in the deception game that Charlie had been playing so well.

Charlie jumped in to rescue me. "Constantine Spiro was unique. A true scholar and a man for all seasons," he said in his most earnest voice. "Well, gentlemen, if that's all, I have an important board meeting to get to."

The manager thumbed through the papers in the file. "I think we're complete," he said.

"Good. I need to confer with my nephew a minute outside and then he can come back in to collect his friend . . . our friend."

Outside in the parking lot, Charlie yanked at his tie.

"Man, that was more fun than Fourth of July firecrackers," he said. "I love to screw the bureaucracy any chance I get."

"D----o you think we could get in trouble for what we did?"

"No way. All those official papers and carbon copies will go in a file somewhere, never to be seen again. I've covered government agencies for a long time. A bunch of real skullduggery goes on that never sees the light of day, but our little fudge-a-ma-roo is harmless, virtually kid stuff in the grand scheme of things."

Charlie took off his coat. "You don't think I laid it on too thick in there, do you?"

"I almost b----elieved you myself. I thought the guy was going to salute when you said that about the cannons roaring."

Charlie laughed. He tugged on the handle of the badly dented door on his Falcon.

"Well, I must get to my important board meeting . . . at the Poor & Hungry. A shuffleboard meeting, to be exact. I hope our friend in there doesn't see this fancy executive car of mine."

The Falcon sputtered blue smoke. Charlie saluted as he drove out of the lot.

* * *

The familiar duffel bag with its stenciled lettering sat on the manager's desk.

Constantine Spiro
SS *Patrick Henry*

"Here we are, Mr. Vollmer. My instructions dictated that this is exactly how the remains were to be presented." He pushed the duffel bag and its contents forward on his desk.

"You'll see that the urn inside is our basic brass model, simple but elegant. No engraving, as specified by the deceased. You'll note that the urn's top is sealed with a special tape that holds well and can be reused many times."

The manager handed me copies of the papers Charlie had signed.

"Once again, you should be aware that I followed specific

instructions as to the urn and the urn's contents." The more the manager talked, the more it seemed he was apologizing for something.

"The c----ontents are only Mr. Spiro's ashes. Right?"

The manager changed to more of a funeral-home voice. "The contents and the presentation are exactly as specified by the deceased. I wish you well."

I took the way he said those words to mean it was time for me to leave and stop asking questions.

Walking to the car, I held the duffel bag in my right arm and tight to my chest, the way my football coach taught me to carry the ball so I didn't fumble.

The afternoon Memphis heat made the soles of my shoes sticky on the asphalt, but I was going to put up my convertible top. I didn't want the sun or anything else to harm my special cargo in the passenger seat. Mr. Spiro would be safe and sound until I could find my way to New Orleans and then on to his final resting place at the Mouth of the Mississippi River.

I had a long way to go, but finally I was making good progress.

Chapter 6

Not many people who have jobs starting at four in the morning showed up for work an hour early, but I was so excited about my coming trip that I found it difficult to sleep. Before it was time to clock in, I did some typing on one of the typewriters at the copydesk.

Anytime Mr. Spiro prepared for one of his trips where he would catch a ride on a towboat on the river, he would announce that he was going to prepare his "ship's manifest," a list of final chores and items he wanted to be sure to take with him. I typed a manifest for my trip.

> Change of clothes
> Bathroom stuff
> Book
> M volume of the encyclopedia
> Road map

Snacks
Typewriter
Get gas
Get oil changed
Cash last 3 paychecks at bank
Write letter
Hide urn in trunk

Typing the manifest put a realness to my plans. I pulled the sheet of paper out of the typewriter and went over it. I crossed out the *M* volume of the encyclopedia that had the two full pages about the Mississippi River. I would have time during the weekend to copy the two pages on my typewriter. It would give me something to do until my departure on Monday morning.

I finished my Friday copyboy duties early, which gave me time to play my secret headline game with the stories coming off the news wires. When I suspected a particular story would be chosen for the newspaper, I would write a headline for it on a separate piece of paper. I liked to check my headline against the real one that came out in the newspaper to see how close I was. A few times I had managed to match the real headline word for word.

* * *

Waiting outside the managing editor's office in a chair gave me a good view of everything going on in the newsroom.

The head copy clerk, a skinny older man with a cluster of keys jangling on his belt, came in with the first sack of mail from the post office and threw the canvas bag on the big work table. The city hall reporter grabbed the mailbag to dump out the contents.

"Get your grubby paws off that," the clerk said.

"I'm expecting something important from the Washington bureau."

"I don't care if you're expecting Marilyn Monroe. Keep your hands off the mail until I get it sorted in the boxes."

The reporter walked away, then turned back to the head copy clerk.

"Marilyn Monroe is dead, you old nincompoop."

"So is Babe Ruth." The clerk smiled with his comeback even though it didn't make any sense.

A kind of unwritten chain of command existed in the newsroom. Only the senior copy clerk, never a copyboy, could talk back to a reporter. The city editor could yell at a reporter but not at a copy editor. The managing editor could yell—and did— at most everybody in the newsroom, especially on deadline. The editor stayed in his office and out of the way.

"Morning, Vic," the managing editor said. "So, what did you decide?"

"I'd like to k----eep working while I go to school."

"Good enough then. I'll put in the paperwork and get you on the schedule."

"I have a trip already p----lanned for next week, but I could be b----ack by Friday and start then."

The managing editor was already deep into the stack of newspapers on his desk, muttering and making circles with a red grease pencil.

"Fine, see you then. Next Friday."

I wanted to thank him or, at the least, give him a nod and a smile, but with some people those things seemed to be wasted effort.

The copydesk had finished with the first edition. I walked up to Charlie with a batch of wire copy as he flipped through the morning newspaper.

"D----id you have a chance—" Charlie didn't let me finish. He was amped up from coffee and the rush of the deadline.

"Done. My friend Ray Patton knows you're coming down to see him. I gave him a quick rundown about you and the reason for your trip."

"Thanks. My p----lan is to leave Monday morning at four."

Charlie counted in his head.

"Eight hours down there, so you should get there before Ray gets off work, and I use that term loosely. This Monday is Labor Day, but Ray assures me he'll be at work." Charlie handed me a slip of paper with a name, address, and phone number on it.

I was anxious to learn a little more about the person in New Orleans who was going to help me find the mouth of the river.

"How g----ood a friend is your friend?"

"Let's put it like this. If I was in a jam and needed someone at my back, I would want it to be the General. You'll like him and if he doesn't treat you right, I told him I'd dun him for the twenty bucks he owes me."

"Where d----o you know him from?"

"The General is an old newspaper buddy from Arkansas who somehow talked his way into the cushy job as the outdoor editor for the *Times-Picayune*."

"Was he a general in the Army or something?"

"No, but it's one of my favorite stories. I was an eyewitness." Charlie folded the newspaper he was reading and changed to his storytelling voice. Asking Charlie a question was like turning on a faucet, especially when he had one of his good stories to tell and he was off deadline.

"Ray Patton was a police reporter at the paper in Little Rock. The best reporter the paper had. One day the city editor told Ray to go get this certain story he had heard about that involved something bad a police officer might have done. Ray came back and told the city editor that he had checked into it and there was no story there."

Charlie stood for the benefit of the other copy editors around the rim who also liked to hear his stories.

"The city editor shouts so everyone in the newsroom can hear: 'I'm the damn city editor and if I say there's a story, then there's a story.' Ray shouts back just as loud, 'Well, I'm the damn reporter and if I say there's no story there, then there's no story there.'"

Charlie moved his chair away from the copydesk for a big finish.

"The city editor completely lost it. Started slobbering and spitting, turned red and stuck a finger in Ray's face. 'You may be a Patton, but you're not a general. You're fired.'"

At that point, Charlie had the copydesk's full attention.

"Ray clicks his heels together, does this animated salute and says, 'Sir, yes, sir.' He does an about-face, smiles to everyone who's watching, and walks right out of the newsroom to a round of applause. He's been called 'General' by his friends ever since."

Charlie's story and the way he told it had the copy editors laughing.

"I've got some news." I was speaking to Charlie, but I wanted everyone on the copydesk to hear. "I'm g----oing to keep my copyboy job in the mornings while I go to school."

"Hey, that's great." Charlie turned to the copydesk.

"Everybody hear that? Young Victor here is going to labor in the ranks of the proletariat while he goes to college."

Some of the copy editors nodded, noses in their mugs of coffee.

"This calls for a penny toss," Charlie said, reaching into his pocket. "Take this penny and see if you can stick it in the ceiling for good luck."

I took the penny and held it between two fingers and my thumb, getting a good feel of how to balance it. With a motion that was part underhand and part sidearm, I spun the coin out of my hand and up to the penny-laden ceiling.

The copy editors looked up. The penny's edge hit squarely and then disappeared into the soft acoustic tile.

"Jeez Louise, we'll never see that penny again," Charlie said.

The coin toss was exactly what I needed.

"See you g----uys next Friday."

"Don't do anything I wouldn't do," Charlie said. "Or at least don't get caught at it."

I pushed the down arrow on the old elevator, but didn't feel like waiting for the clunky contraption. I took the stairs, two at a time.

My journey would begin in a little more than two days. I was confident I was going to reach New Orleans before that stick I tossed in the river did.

★ ★ ★

Even though it was a holiday weekend, my father was out of town on business, so it was just my mother and me for supper on Sunday night. She talked about the sales that would take place after Labor Day and how we would go shopping Tuesday for new clothes for college. I tried to make my nods noncommittal.

After helping with the dishes, I went upstairs to my room and began typing—words of my own, not a list and not somebody else's words copied from a book. A letter to my parents.

> I know you are going to be mad at me and I can't really blame you, but I hope you understand that this is something I have to do on my own and I can't wait any longer.
>
> I am leaving to take Mr. Spiro's ashes to the Mouth of the Mississippi River like I promised him I would. I have a friend of a friend down there who is going to help me find the right spot at the end of the river.
>
> I should be back by Wednesday night or sometime on Thursday at the very latest.
>
> You don't need to worry about me. I borrowed a road map and you know how good I am at reading maps.
>
> I have another thing to tell you. I've decided for sure I'm not going to play baseball at Southwestern and will continue working my copyboy job at the newspaper while I go to school. I like working at the paper. And everybody there says I'm good at what I do.
>
> I'm excited about keeping my promise to Mr. Spiro and I hope you won't be too upset with me when I get back. I have to be at work on Friday morning at four o'clock.
>
> Victor
>
> P.S. I got the oil changed in my car and I'm taking extra money in case I need it, but I probably won't.

My mother was still a little put out with me for taking the copyboy job at the start of the summer without consulting her first. She said it ruined any chance of us taking a summer family vacation. Mr. Spiro was the one who had called my attention to the help-wanted ad in the newspaper. I applied for it and got it all on my own. My father told my mother that getting the job showed initiative and that he was proud of me. My parents started arguing, and I left the room. I didn't even bother to go back and do my usual eavesdropping.

I reread my letter several times. In my head, I could see my mother reading what I had written and then calling my father on the telephone and then they would start arguing. I would be long gone.

Chapter 7

My parents' bedroom was on the first floor, but there was little chance my mother would hear me leave so early in the morning. If she happened to hear anything, she would think it was just me going to work.

My gym bag was packed. I took the five twenty-dollar-bills I had gotten from cashing my three paychecks and rolled them tight with a rubber band. I didn't like to carry that much money on me, so I put the roll of bills in the bottom of the gym bag under my clothes.

In the kitchen, I grabbed an apple and a sleeve of saltine crackers. Even though I usually raided the pantry and refrigerator several times a day, I felt like a thief in my parents' kitchen so early in the morning. As much as I wanted to, I didn't take the new bag of Oreo cookies.

I checked on Mr. Spiro's duffel bag and urn, which I had wedged in the trunk next to the spare tire in my small Austin-Healey Sprite. Before I cranked the engine, I went over the manifest for my trip that I had transferred to my head. I had forgotten something. My typewriter. I sneaked back to my room for it, glad that the thick carpet kept the stairs from squeaking.

I didn't plan on doing any typing on the trip, but I felt better with it sitting there in the floorboard of my car. Doing things without a sound reason sometimes just felt good.

* * *

I knew how to cross into the state of Mississippi by taking Highway 61. That was the route we always took to our summer cabin on Moon Lake, but leaving Memphis on Highway 51 was new to me. I stopped by the newspaper to check the oversized city map on the wall in the newsroom.

The copyboy who was scheduled to replace me had not made it to work yet. I paired up some of the stories from the international wires so he wouldn't be too far behind when he arrived. Stories were coming out of Southeast Asia at a fast clip. The newspaper was full of stories with Vietnam and Cambodia datelines and news about the war.

A story from Caracas, Venezuela, caught my eye. A tropical depression had formed in the lower Caribbean near the island of Barbados. The storm's track would put it roughly three hundred miles east of Cuba at midday. I matched it with another wire story from Miami, which said the National Weather Service had issued a weather alert for Florida's Atlantic coast due to the storm.

I checked the national weather wire. New Orleans was sunny

and clear with a high temperature expected in the mid-eighties.

I imagined a fake one-column headline:

VICTOR'S TRIP WILL ENJOY CLEAR SKIES

Not my best work and wouldn't rate a penny toss, but I was in a hurry.

* * *

On South Bellevue at a few minutes before five o'clock, I passed the guitar-shaped gates of Elvis Presley's home. Even at the early hour, a dozen or so people stood outside the iron gate with the musical notes on it.

Mr. Spiro and I talked about Elvis once after I asked him what he thought about the guy as a singer. Mr. Spiro said that popular music was not one of his interests but went on to say that it appeared that Mr. Presley had found "his way." I asked what it meant exactly that someone had found the "way" and how a person could be sure the way he had chosen was right for him.

That's when Mr. Spiro first told me about Nietzsche and the guy in the cave named Zarathustra, not that I understood much of what the story was about. Mr. Spiro had a way of putting extra emphasis on important things by the tone in his voice: "This is *my* way. What is *your* way? *The* way does not exist. Thus spake Zarathustra."

When Mr. Spiro said certain things, it was like the words should be up on a billboard somewhere with lights flashing. I asked him to explain exactly what Zarathustra was talking about.

Mr. Spiro said, "If I show you my path, it is only my path. The one and only path does not exist. Thus, we are on our own to find the path that best suits us."

My classmates liked to punch in their favorite songs on jukeboxes. I could punch in Mr. Spiro's words in my head without spending a dime.

South Bellevue turned into Highway 51. Whitehaven in Memphis turned into Southaven in Mississippi. South of the little town of Hernando, I pulled over and got out the Esso road map I had borrowed from the glove box in my mother's car. I unfolded it on the steering wheel. The sun was up enough to let me trace with my finger the highway's red squiggly line leading all the way to New Orleans.

Senatobia. Grenada. Itta Bena. Winona. Kosciusko. The names of the small towns in Mississippi sounded like names from a foreign country. I spotted a more familiar name—Coldwater— the town that Mam had moved back to when she stopped working for us.

My mother said we didn't need Mam anymore to cook for us or help take care of me. Plus, since we had the world's greatest central-vacuum system, it would be easier to keep the house clean. Mam had this special way of using baking soda and a broom to clean rugs. I would have put her up any day against the world's greatest vacuum cleaner. For months I kept asking my mother if we could go to Coldwater to visit Mam, but she soon got fed up with my pestering and told me not to talk about it again.

I wasn't sure if Mam moved back to her people in Coldwater because she didn't have a job anymore or because she didn't like the way some people treated her in Memphis. She had to ride in a certain spot on the bus and she couldn't go to the zoo, except on certain days or when she was with me. A few times I even heard her called a bad name. It was all I could do not to bust somebody a good one when that happened.

If I had time on my way back home from New Orleans, I was going to stop in the little town of Coldwater and try to pay a visit to Mam if I could find her. My trip was for what Mr. Spiro asked me to do, but it wouldn't hurt at the end for me to get a little pleasure of my own by seeing Mam again.

★ ★ ★

Driving with my top down in the city meant the smells were mostly fumes from trucks and buses, unless you were lucky enough to be passing Leonard's Pit Barbecue on South Bellevue.

Outside the city, the air had various odors depending on where you were on the highway. If there was cotton growing in a field, it smelled one way and if the field had been plowed recently or if the farmer was cutting hay, it smelled another way. Cattle in a pasture gave off another smell, but even that wasn't so bad knowing how everything was fresh.

The temperature also changed depending on if you dropped down a little to go through a river valley or went up a hill, not that there were many hills on Highway 51. In the cars my parents drove, the windows were always up with either the heater or the air conditioner blowing and I never paid much attention to everything going on outside. Driving with my top down was almost the same as walking, feeling like I was a part of everything instead of passing through it in a tunnel.

My mother refused to ride in my little car that my father gave me for my seventeenth birthday. She told everybody, even if they didn't ask, that it was so low to the ground that it reminded her of a ground sled that her father would pull behind his horses. I also overheard her tell my father when they were having a fight that she knew the only reason he bought me the new sports car in the first place was to impress his friends. Anytime my mother said hateful things a big argument would start and my father would end up walking out of the room without saying anything. Another out-of-town business trip soon would follow.

Stale thoughts. I was on my first road trip completely on my own, and all I could think was stale thoughts. The speed limit on the highway was fifty-five miles an hour, but I kicked it up to sixty to blow those thoughts out of my head.

To keep myself company, I typed the first words of Hemingway's book on the steering wheel with my fingers:

He was an old man who fished alone in a skiff in the Gulf Stream . . .

* * *

The morning rush-hour traffic in Jackson, Mississippi, was lighter than I expected when I reached the city limits, and then I remembered it was a holiday. My fuel gauge showed a little less than half a tank remaining, but it would be a good time to fill up and take a short break from the wind noise. My windshield also needed cleaning in the worst way.

I spotted an Esso station with a picnic table to one side in a grassy area. An attendant in a gray uniform met me at the pumps. He appeared to be older than me, but not by much. The flat-topped Esso hat that came with the uniform was the kind only an adult would like wearing. He wore it tilted back on his head so it wouldn't mess up his swirl of hair in front.

"What can I do you for?" he said.

"Ch----eck the oil and fill it with high-test, please." I liked to have the choice of whether to say "high-test" or "ethyl," and would decide at the last possible second which word to use. If you stutter, there's nothing better than having options.

"And I'll try to do something 'bout them Mississippi lovebugs all over your windshield and headlamps. You must a been driving a while," the attendant said.

"What's a lovebug?"

"Them are those little bugs that do it in the air just 'fore they get smushed. That's the way I want to go, man. How 'bout you?"

I didn't know how to answer the question.

The attendant's name—Fred—was on an oval patch sewn on his uniform. When I was younger I secretly thought about working at a service station with my name displayed on my shirt so I would never have to say it if someone asked. I could simply point to my chest. I liked it when I played sports in a uniform that let me be a number and not a person with a name.

The picnic table was a good place to spread out the map and check my progress. Without the wind noise in my ears, I heard myself munching on my apple. I took my little finger and measured distance-to-go and distance-traveled on the map. I was making good time. Reading maps was one of my favorite things to do. I liked the idea of knowing that my body was actually at a certain place on the planet Earth but also was at a spot on a paper map that I could put my finger on. I thought of the map as fiction, and my body as nonfiction. Mr. Spiro had told me that often there was more truth in fiction than nonfiction, like there was more truth in a good painting than in a photograph. The more I thought about that, the more right he seemed to be.

"Oil's good. Gas is three dollars, six cents. Just give me three bucks and we'll call it even," Fred said.

"I have change," I said.

"Don't like to fool with it. Three bucks is close enough."

He pulled a rag from his back pocket and rubbed hard on the windshield.

"I can't get all them squished lovebugs off, but I got a trick if you've a mind to try it. Go buy a Coca-Cola at the machine, and I'll pour it on the windshield and let them bugs soak a spell. They'll come right off with that Coca-Cola, slick as a whistle."

The windshield was clean enough for me.

"It's not bad. You g----ot most of them off."

"Suit yourself. Mind if I ask where you're headed to?"

"N----ew Orleans."

"How 'bout a good sidekick for the trip?" Fred pushed his cap even farther back on his head. "I get off at noon and get paid. I could help a little with gas money, and don't worry, I'll be getting shed of this uniform."

"No room." I pointed to the typewriter in the floorboard.

"You can put that thing in the trunk."

"Trunk's full."

"Suit yourself, but you're missing out," he said. "I been to New Orleans lots of times and could show you things I bet you never seen before."

"I have some b----usiness to take care of and I'm kind of on a t----ight schedule." I had heard my father say "tight schedule" many times, but the words had a phony sound the way they came out of my mouth.

"There's a new freeway to New Orleans that ain't all the way open yet, but I know how to get on it and buzz us down there. How 'bout it?"

I ended the conversation by shaking my head and getting in my car.

"Okay, Mr. Tight Schedule. Go on and take care of your business with your lovebugs and your fancy little car." Fred slapped his shop rag against his leg and walked away from the pumps.

Easing back into the traffic on Highway 51 South, I tried to think what Fred might have had against my car. Anyway, my typewriter in the floorboard had proven useful.

* * *

Traffic was even lighter south of Jackson, hardly any trucks. Signs pointed to the new interstate highway, but the new road didn't show on my map yet. Highway 51 was my route and I was sticking to it. I was more than two hundred miles from Memphis, closer to New Orleans than to home. Mr. Spiro traveled the world and I wanted to be like him, to have the confidence to hop on a boat and go to any place I could think of, but my feeling of being isolated and all on my own was coming back stronger than ever on the empty highway and farther from home than I had ever been by myself.

The longer I drove, the more the idea of a sidekick appealed to me, even though Fred's plans in New Orleans, whatever they happened to be, were likely to be far different from mine.

I felt so alone that I halfway considered going back to the Esso station to see if Fred was still interested in a ride, but I did have to deal with a "tight schedule," phony as that phrase sounded coming out of my mouth. I searched in my head for comforting words from Mr. Spiro, but all that came to me was a sentence from the book about the giant fish towing the old man and his skiff far out into the gulf:

He looked across the sea and knew how alone he was now.

At least I didn't have the sharks to worry about. Only the pairs of lovebugs popping against my windshield.

Chapter 8

Crossing the state line into Louisiana shortly after noon put me ahead of the schedule I kept in my head. I was hungry, but I started thinking that I had never gone into a restaurant by myself and ordered a meal on my own. I opened the sleeve of saltine crackers with my teeth and munched away while I drove.

The crackers didn't last but a few miles. My mouth was so dry it felt like I had eaten a package of sandpaper. In between two small towns, I spotted a Coca-Cola machine outside a laundromat. My first baseball coach in high school told the team that carbonated drinks would ruin your health and keep you from being a good ball player. If he caught anybody drinking anything made of fizz water, it was an automatic one-game suspension. The coach was long gone, but I still had a hard time convincing myself it was okay to drink a Coca-Cola.

I fished a dime out of my pocket and slid it into the coin slot.

The bottle made a racket as it wormed its way down inside the machine to the opening at my knees. I looked to see if anyone was watching, flipped off the bottle cap in the opener, and took a quick sip. Then a long one. The one good thing about not drinking a soft drink for so many years was that when you finally did break down and have one, the taste was all new and exciting.

★ ★ ★

The map was open beside me, one end tucked into the fold of the bucket seat so it would stay flat. The nonfiction was the hours I had spent on the road. The fiction was the short distance of inches I had moved on the map.

At the town of Ponchatoula, Louisiana, Highway 51 intersected with Highway 22. A sign pointed to the Lake Pontchartrain Causeway. My map told me the long bridge was a quicker route to downtown New Orleans, where the *Times-Picayune* was located according to Charlie. From my father's airplane, the gigantic lake had always seemed more like an ocean with a tiny ribbon of a bridge strung tightly across it. Now, with the sun hot on the right side of my face, it just looked like a lonely road on the water that went on and on to nowhere.

The air had a damp smell as I drove, making me think I should be crossing the lake in a boat instead of in a car. The lower speed limit and the 24-mile straight shot across the water gave me the opportunity to type out a new manifest in my head:

Find the Times-Picayune
Talk to the General
Make my way to the river
Locate the mouth
Spread the ashes

Was it really that easy?

Would I have to rent a boat to go out on the river?

Could a seventeen-year-old even rent a boat?

It was already the middle of the afternoon. Where would I spend the night?

What if I was too late and the General had already left the newspaper for the day? Charlie had not given me his home address.

Simple and logical questions bombarded me like the lovebugs that were still hitting my windshield. The closer I got to my destination, the more the questions jumped out at me. Is this the way it was when an older person took a trip? The closer you got to where you were going, the more complicated everything became? The typewriter in my head had no answers.

★ ★ ★

I crossed Lake Pontchartrain in thirty minutes. Finding the *Times-Picayune* on Poydras Street took three times that long. I had to stop at two different gas stations to ask directions and "Poydras" wasn't one of my favorite words to say. I had never heard it pronounced and new words like that needed a little time to settle in my brain before I was any good at getting them out.

Driving in New Orleans was not the same as driving in Memphis, and not for the reason that all the streets were new to me. Car horns were louder and drivers much more likely to use them in New Orleans. I got honked at anytime I didn't challenge for position in a lane in my little car. When I did try to change lanes on Canal Street, cars and trucks wouldn't let me. My father once told me that Canal Street was the widest street in the world. As far as I was concerned, it was also the scariest to drive on.

A man in a truck swerved in front of me. I honked at him. It was the first time I had ever used my horn in traffic. I didn't like the shrill sound it made, almost like a hurt animal. The horn also reminded me of one of my out-of-control screams.

Sweat rolled down into my eyes as I pulled my car into a parking spot on the street around the corner from the newspaper building. I put the top up, stuffed my gym bag in the trunk, and locked the lid. Locking the doors wasn't of much use since the car had flimsy sliding windows that anyone could open easily from the outside. Anyway, the only thing in the front was my heavy typewriter that someone would have a hard time lifting from the floorboard if they had in mind to steal it.

Two women in the lobby of the *Times-Picayune* sat behind a long counter and on both sides of a telephone switchboard where they pushed and pulled different-colored plugs attached to cords. When they let go of a cord, it snapped back into its hole like a frightened snake.

"T-P, how may I direct your call?"

The two women spoke the words in one breath over and over, paying no attention to me. I had to interrupt them by raising my hand like I was in a classroom. The woman on the right leaned toward me, lifting her earpiece.

"Help you?"

"I . . . n----eed to see the General?"

"General? General who?"

I was rattled. I couldn't remember the real name of Charlie Roker's friend that was written on the piece of paper in my gym bag. Only that he was "the General."

The operator went back to pulling and pushing plugs.

"F----orgot . . . can't remember his name, but he's like the general of the outdoors."

The other operator leaned around her side of the switchboard.

"Are you talking 'bout Ray Patton?"

"That's it." My voice was too loud, like I had gotten the correct answer on a television quiz show.

"Newsroom. Second floor." The operator pointed to an elevator on the other side of the large lobby.

The newspaper offices at the *Times-Picayune* sounded and looked much like the newsroom at the *Memphis Press-Scimitar*. Typewriters and Teletype machines clattered away. Reporters and editors shouted to be heard over police scanners and shortwave radios. Pneumatic tubes hissed and sucked air in different parts of the room.

At the *Press-Scimitar* this late in the day, the newsroom would be empty. The *Times-Picayune* was a morning newspaper, so everything was going full blast late in the afternoon, even on a holiday. I didn't know anyone, but I felt almost comfortable in the busy but strange newsroom.

A man, surrounded at his desk by three telephones of different colors, chewed on a fat unlit cigar. To no one in particular, he yelled: "Copy!"

A guy a little older than me rushed over with an empty pneumatic tube in his hand, grabbed the sheets of paper and rolled them into the cylinder. I caught up to the copyboy as he put the tube in the hole to be whisked away.

"Is Ray P----atton here?"

"You mean 'the General'?"

I nodded.

"Sports department. Against the back wall," the copyboy

said. "His desk is the one with the gator on top. He's probably there . . . just can't see him for all his crapola."

I heard the clacking of the typewriter before I saw it. Ray Patton sat sideways at his desk, hammering on the keys with two fingers faster than anyone I had ever seen. The typewriter sat on its own metal stand. The General held a telephone receiver to his ear by scrunching up his shoulder. He glanced up and nodded for me to sit in a nearby chair. The telephone conversation was one-sided with the General saying, "Tell me more about that," and "I see," and "Spell that for me," in between his quick laughs.

The small stuffed alligator, resting on top of a hodgepodge of books and telephone directories, had a tiny umbrella in its mouth from the Sho Bar. A "My Name Is ___" badge was stuck on the head of the dried-up animal. "Blaze Starr" was written in on the name badge with a red marker. Fishing lures of every shape and color dangled from the spines of books, mostly telephone directories. A coffee mug in bad need of a washing was adorned with a quote:

May God have mercy upon my enemies, because I won't. — General George S. Patton

"Hold on," he said to me as he hung up the receiver. "Let me get this down on paper while it's fresh."

The General blazed away on the typewriter with two fingers, faster than I could type with all ten. I gazed around the busy room.

"All right, then," the General said, jerking the paper and carbon out of his typewriter. "I'd say you have to be one Victor Vollmer from Memphis, Tennessee." We shook hands. Anytime I got away without having to introduce myself was a big plus for me.

"Roker said I could expect you this afternoon. Glad you made it. You must have left Memphis in the wee hours."

"Four o'clock."

This was the time for the small talk that came so easy to most people when they were talking to strangers for the first time, but chatting was like a foreign language to me. The General saw he would need to be the one to get our conversation going.

"So, how's our Rocket Roker doing?" I had never heard Charlie referred to as Rocket but didn't ask about it. I wanted to get on with my business.

"He's g----ood. Charlie said you were the p----erson who might could help me find the Mouth of the Mississippi River."

The General smiled.

"The Rocket warned me that you weren't much on chit-chat. I guess I'm your man, although we need to talk a little more about exactly the place that you have in mind."

The General rearranged some papers on his desk and then rose from his chair. He appeared to be of average height sitting down, but he was tall. Taller than my father.

"Let's get out of here before somebody finds some more work for me to do," he said. The General tapped the stuffed alligator on the head. "Good night, Miss Starr." He pulled an old and cracked typewriter cover from his desk drawer and covered his machine. I liked people who took care of their typewriters.

Fifteen minutes went by before we managed to get out of the building. If the General didn't stop to talk to someone first, likely as not that person would stop and want to joke with him. The General had something to say to everyone he passed. Charlie said the General was a good reporter and I could see why. Everybody wanted to talk and joke around.

The General walked over to the switchboard in the lobby.

"I'm gone for the day, my PBX lovelies. Take a message, as they say." The two ladies smiled at the General as they pushed and pulled their switchboard cords.

We stepped onto the sidewalk. The tall buildings put the street in the shade this late in the day.

"First order of business is for us to go have a beer," the General said. "You are eighteen aren't you?"

I shook my head. "N----ot for a few months yet."

"Okay, cancel that. The first order of business is for *me* to have a beer and *you* to watch," the General said. "Charlie wouldn't want me to lead you down the road to debauchery. He'll want to be in charge of that himself."

We came to my car parked at the sidewalk meter.

"Can't leave this little ragtop here," the General said. "It'll be sliced up like a watermelon as soon as the sun sets. You can park it in the employee lot and we'll take my truck."

"Is there a ch----ance of me getting to the Mouth of the Mississippi River before it gets too dark?" Figuring out a way to hurry someone without being too much of a pain was another talking skill that I lacked. My question was met with silence.

The General leaned on the front fender of my car. He folded his arms, like he was telling me to slow down without having to say any words.

"A couple of things, Son Vic from Memphis." Even though he wasn't a real general, he talked straight at you and firm like generals did in the movies.

"First thing. Charlie told me to take good care of you while you were down here. Second, we need to take a time out to talk about this mouth-of-the-river thing you are so set on. It may be a little more complicated than what you had in mind."

Umpires liked to call pitchers and coaches together before the start of a game to go over the ground rules. The General was doing the same thing with me. He was telling me in his own way to slow down.

"Sorry," I said. "I know I'm b----ad about trying to go too fast. I've been thinking hard about the mouth of the river and getting this close to it probably makes me get in too b----ig of a hurry."

"Don't worry. We'll get it all worked out, but I can assure you that twilight is no time to start messing around with the mighty Mississippi."

I liked the way the General listened to me and then explained exactly what was on his mind. I hoped we could get along and that he would like me eventually, if I could slow myself down and act like a regular person.

"M----aybe the first thing is for me to find a p----lace to stay tonight," I offered, wanting to show the General that I could take a hint and could slow down and think like a grownup. "The only p----lace I know is called The R----oosevelt where my parents stay, and I don't think I have enough money to spend the night there."

"Let me guess," the General said. "You and your family also dine at Commander's Palace and Pascal's Manale and have breakfast at Brennan's."

I nodded.

"Get in your little car, Son Vic, and follow me around to the rear of the building." The General pointed the way. "First thing it looks like we may need to work on is getting that silver spoon dislodged from your throat."

I nodded and got in my car. I could take a hint.

Chapter 9

The raw oyster sat on its half shell in a concoction of cocktail sauce and grated horseradish that the General had gone to a lot of pains to mix.

"Are you sure about this?" I balanced the shell to keep the oyster from sliding off. "Th----ese things don't look like they were m----eant to be eaten."

"You only have to get it started and the oyster will do the rest," he said.

I closed my eyes, put the shell to my lips and tilted my head back. The oyster slid into my mouth and escaped down my throat before I could bite into it.

"I think I m----issed it." I coughed.

"Try another one, and this time try to get in at least one good chew."

I might have missed the oyster, but the sauce lingered and

caused my nose to run and my eyes to water. I couldn't open the little packages of two crackers fast enough. The General ate his dozen oysters and then helped me with most of mine.

Customers of all shapes and sizes packed Felix's Oyster Bar. New Orleans was certainly in the South, but the accents here were different than in Memphis, and people acted like they were at a party even though there didn't seem to be an official party of any kind going on. The General called the bartenders and oyster shuckers by name. Most of the talk up and down the bar had to do with the weather in the Atlantic, what kind of fish were biting, and the quality of the seafood.

A large bearded man slapped the General on the back.

"You need to remind everybody in your column that it's the month to start eating oysters again," he said. They shook hands.

"That's an old wives' tale," the General told the man. "Probably started by one of your many old wives."

The bearded man laughed. "You think that storm in the Atlantic might mess with us over this way?"

"Not likely, but I'd say the East Coast is puckered up real tight about now."

The bearded man laughed again and continued talking to customers up and down the bar.

"What's so special about September and oysters?" I asked the General. My mouth burned so much I could hardly feel it. I wondered if hot sauce might be good for my stuttering since I had lost all feeling around my tongue except for the burning sensation.

"Some say you're not supposed to eat raw shellfish in any month that doesn't have the letter *r*. I eat 'em year-round, sometimes for breakfast."

The General ran his hand through his thick head of hair. "See this lush pasture up here? That's what you get from eating raw oysters all twelve months of the year."

When I had just met somebody it was hard for me to decide if what was said was meant to be a joke. I was getting the hang of it already with the General.

"I think I'm sufficiently sophonsified," the General said. I had never heard that word, even from Mr. Spiro or the copydesk chief. "Let's head on back. I think the best thing is for you to spend the night at my place. It's not the Roosevelt by any stretch, but the price is right."

The General said his goodbyes and put a twenty-dollar bill on the counter.

"It's quiet at my place so we can talk. I know you're anxious to start learning more about where your quest seems to be leading you."

Mr. Spiro was always good at knowing what was going on inside my head. So was the General, and I had just met him. I also liked the word "quest." It was a Mr. Spiro kind of word.

★ ★ ★

The General had parked at a service station where he had given one of the attendants a dollar to watch his truck, but when we started walking back a different way, I had an idea the General had something else in mind. The sidewalks became more crowded the longer we walked. People strolled in the middle of the street with drinks and bottles in their hands and dared cars to hit them.

"Have you ever been to the French Quarter?" the General asked.

"Only driving through in the day." I had the feeling I was going to get a good look at the French Quarter by night.

We turned onto Bourbon Street, the busiest and loudest street yet. I couldn't remember any place like this in Memphis, except for the time six years ago when Mam and I found ourselves on Beale Street at night in downtown Memphis.

Men at the doors on Bourbon Street wore shiny suits and smoked thin cigarettes. They opened and closed the doors, inviting passersby in to get a peak of the show and enjoy the air conditioning that spilled out like when you opened a refrigerator door. I looked in a few of the doors and saw twirling colored lights and ladies dancing on stages in front of walls made of mirrors. Their dancing costumes were mostly sequins and feathers that didn't cover up much. Small bands with loud horns played on the stages. As we walked past the opening and closing doors, the sounds grew confusing, like spinning the tuner knob on a loud radio.

The hawkers and their swinging doors went on as far as I could see down crowded Bourbon Street.

"So, tell me what you think about the French Quarter at night."

"It's lively."

"That's one way to put it." The General walked with his hands in his pocket. "A little of it goes a long way, if you ask me, but I know that people enjoy a peek into a fantasy world. And remember that's what it is, Son Vic. Pure fantasy."

The General never looked in the open doors or made eye contact with the men in suits, who seemed to know there was no need for them to say anything to him. The walk down Bourbon Street appeared to be for my benefit.

"You've been up a while," the General said. "We probably should get you to your berth." The General used nautical terms like Mr. Spiro, one of the many things I liked about my New Orleans guide and new friend.

We weaved through the crowds on the sidewalks and streets. The noise of the French Quarter followed us all the way to the truck. I remembered the General backing out of the service station, but not much after that.

* * *

Horn blasts rattled through my head. Towboat horns, I decided. Not the jazz horns of the French Quarter. My gym bag had been my pillow in the truck and had given me a bad crick in my neck.

"How long have we been stopped here?" I massaged my neck with both hands.

"About an hour. You went straight off to la-la land," said the General, his eyes closed but not asleep. "Let's go down and get us some bona fide shut-eye."

"Where are we?"

"At the river. Where I live."

The Mississippi River was wider here than it was at Memphis and the boats larger. Ocean-going freighters were docked on both sides of the river. The cranes that loaded the massive ships resembled a forest of skinny trees made out of metal. There was no nighttime on this part of the river. The effect of the huge floodlights on the docks was doubled by their reflection in the water. Much like the French Quarter, this part of the river didn't seem to sleep.

The General led me across cobblestones onto a wooden boardwalk to an old barge tied to pilings sticking up out of the river. A narrow gangplank made of a heavy metal mesh led onto the barge.

"Watch your step," the General said. "This can be a little hard to navigate if you're asleep or otherwise encumbered."

The dull-red barge with its sliding metal roof looked like any of the barges up and down the Mississippi River that I liked to watch from my father's airplane. Part of the metal roof had been replaced by the kind of glass panels used in greenhouses. Plants and flowers growing in cans and buckets dotted the top of the barge.

"You really live here?"

"I really do," he said. "This barge has been a residence for more than thirty years, when the river wasn't so crowded. I moved aboard it six years ago. You can't dock barges anymore and live on them, but this one was grandfathered in."

The General opened a hatch in the metal deck.

"You've never been rocked to sleep like the river can rock you," he said. "Let me have your bag."

He backed down through the hatch. Lights came on, shining up through the skylights.

"You have permission to come aboard," he yelled from below.

When my father flew over the river, I made a game of counting the number of barges that made up a tow. The record was 22. If you look at something from high above, you can't tell the size. The General's barge was huge.

Down inside the floating box of metal, the furniture and the rugs looked as nice as the ones my mother had bought for our new house. The light fixtures on the walls and ceiling all matched like they do on submarines in the movies. A large kitchen stove sat in one corner next to a metal sink with a porthole above it.

In the rear of the room was a wooden wall with bookshelves and racks of fishing rods.

"You really live here." It wasn't a question this time. I turned in circles in one spot to try to take in the home floating on the Mississippi River.

"Since you didn't eat many oysters, I'll be happy to fix you a sandwich before you turn in."

"I'm fine. Those oy----sters don't n----eed any company right now." I wasn't sure if the General would get my joke, but he laughed.

"The head is through there." The General pointed to a door in the wooden wall. "You can shower now or wait until the morning."

He opened a chest of drawers, pulled out two sheets and a pillow and began to make up the couch.

"Slept here many a night," he said. "You'll find it plenty comfortable."

"Where will you sleep?"

"I'm behind that long curtain over there." He fluffed a pillow for the couch. "I'm about ready to turn in myself after I take a whiz. I kept us out a little late, but we can get up early in the morning and get our river business done."

I had forgotten to put pajamas on my manifest since I never wore them at home. My white briefs would have to do. I folded my pants and shirt and placed them on the arm of the couch.

A towboat on the river let out a series of short blasts. The General stepped back through the door from the head.

"You might hear the first couple of those, but they won't bother you after that. Sleep well, Son Vic."

With the lights off in the barge, the stars in the Louisiana night sparkled through the windows above. The sheets had a fresh smell that always made me sleep better. New Orleans was humid like Memphis, but the floor of the barge felt cool. The river flowing around the vessel seemed to be a kind of a natural air conditioning.

The General was right about the towboat horns and about being rocked to sleep by the river. I may have heard a few more horn blasts, but that was it. At one point during the night, I thought I heard the General talking to somebody, but then decided it was only the oysters and the hot sauce in my stomach talking back to me.

Chapter 10

Bacon sizzled in a frying pan, reminding me of Mam in our old kitchen in Memphis. When she fried bacon or chicken, the hot grease in the big iron skillet would pop and jump, but it never seemed to bother her. The early morning towboat traffic on the river had increased the gentle rocking of the barge. Sun filtered in at a low angle through the skylights.

I traced in my half-asleep brain the last 24 hours that had taken me from my quiet house in Memphis to a loud New Orleans French Quarter and now to a comfortable home floating on the Mississippi River. Four hundred miles could just as well have been four thousand.

I wondered if my mother had called my father after she read my note. I could imagine her having a hissy fit and then my father telling her to calm down while he looked into it. If there was ever a problem, he always would say he would "look into it."

Things didn't upset him much on the outside, but I had a hunch that wasn't true for his inside.

A woman's voice.

"Shhhhh," the General whispered. "Vic's still sleeping."

I snapped my eyes tight. Light footsteps padded across the barge floor. My shirt and pants were on the far end of the couch. I didn't know how I was going to get dressed with a woman in the room.

More whispers and new smells came from the kitchen. The only thing to do was try to scoot down under the sheet and see if I could pull my clothes over to me with my foot. The cushions soon bunched up, leaving me stuck under the sheet in the middle of the couch in my undershorts.

"That's a strange morning exercise," the General said. "You ever seen an exercise like that, Adrienne?"

"Can't say I have. Looks like fun, sure."

I peeked over the back of the couch to see the General and a woman standing next to him smiling at me. She wore a loose-fitting piece of clothing that could have been either a robe or a dress. Her hair was dark with plenty of curls in it and then I saw that her eyes were just as dark as her hair. The woman was younger than the General, but maybe not by many years. The General turned the bacon in the frying pan with a long fork.

"Say good morning to Adrienne," the General said.

I smiled, nodded, and pulled the sheet up around me.

"*Bonjour*, Vic. Hope I didn't wake you. Welcome to New Orleans."

She pronounced my name "Veek" and New Orleans somehow turned into "Gnaw-leans." I liked the way the words came out of her mouth, like they had a bright coat of paint on them.

"Breakfast'll be ready soon," the General said. "Get your shower, Son Vic, and we'll be waiting with your favorite dish . . . a dozen oysters on the half shell with my special hot sauce." He laughed out loud. "Just kidding."

With the sheet covering me, I gathered up my clothes and gym bag. Through the door on the wooden wall was an oversized bathroom with a claw-foot tub like the one in our old house in Memphis, except this tub had a curtain around it with a big shower head directly above. The ceiling had more skylights in this part of the barge. I took my shower with the morning Louisiana sun shining in on me.

Who was Adrienne? Where did she come from in the middle of the night? And why did the General keep calling me "Son Vic?" Good questions for the shower, where the warm water quickly washed off four hundred miles of Highway 51 South and a night in the French Quarter.

* * *

The big table in the middle of the kitchen had wooden bench seats like a picnic table, but the tabletop itself was gray metal. Strips of thick bacon surrounded a pile of scrambled eggs on a big plate. Another plate held pastries covered with powdered sugar.

The General, in gym shorts and an undershirt, twisted orange halves one by one on a juicer.

Adrienne came through the hatch and down the ladder with a bouquet of fresh flowers in her hand. She filled a glass jar with water, arranged the flowers in it, and put it in the middle of the table.

"How 'bout some *café au lait*, Vic?" Adrienne reached for a black pot on the stove.

"If you mean c----offee, I usually don't drink it."

The General wiped his hands on the towel on his shoulder and got out another mug.

"All right, Son Vic," he said. "Now you know your way around raw oysters and Bourbon Street, so your next lesson is New Orleans coffee."

The General poured steaming milk into the mug from a pan on the stove and an equal part of black coffee that looked like syrup.

"You don't eat them *beignet* without New Orleans coffee," Adrienne said.

"What's a *b----in-y----ey*?" Words that I didn't know how to spell gave me added trouble and I stuttered a little on both syllables, unusual even for me.

"A fried doughnut. French like. I pick 'em up on the way home from work."

The three of us ate breakfast. I didn't realize how hungry I was. The General gave Adrienne a condensed version of the quest that brought me to New Orleans. People who worked at newspapers told their stories the same way that they wrote them, using as few words as possible and leaving out details that didn't add information that wasn't needed for the story.

I had a second cup of coffee with a beignet. The hot milk made the strong coffee go down easier. It tasted more like hot chocolate. Adrienne leaned over the table more than once to brush the white powdered sugar from the beignets off my nose. She and the General kept up a steady conversation that I enjoyed listening to, especially the way Adrienne pronounced her words.

She told me she had met Charlie Roker and how much she liked him. She also referred to Charlie as Rocket. Before I could ask about the nickname, she started telling the General about her Friday night at Commander's Palace and about how much she had made in tips.

"She makes more money waitressing than I do writing the world's most exhilarating prose," the General said.

"You write about fish and duck, and I serve them. We're practically in the same *entreprise*." I could tell she had said the word "enterprise," but her accent made the simple word exciting.

"I'll never be able to get one up on this lady." The General gently squeezed the back of Adrienne's neck.

"So, you're starting college soon, and what about a *cherie*? I bet you have a steady girl in Memphis," Adrienne said.

"N----ot really."

My answer fell flat. It needed something more to prop it up. I could tell that Adrienne wanted to start a conversation.

"I have d----ates for proms and stuff, but I have a hard time talking to girls . . . b----ecause of the way I talk."

Adrienne's reaction was not what I expected. She smiled. I don't know why I brought up the subject of my stuttering. Sometimes my mouth kept going when my brain was thinking something else, but I needed to end with some type of explanation.

"I think I try harder not to stutter around g----irls my age, and that's when my words can get all messed up."

"You just haven't found the right *jeune fille*," Adrienne said. "There's one out there who will like every part of you, sure, including that cute stutter."

Cute stutter? Two words I had never heard together.

Adrienne and the General chattered away. When my mother and father talked to each other, they seemed to have to work extra hard to think of things to say, but my new friends on the barge went back and forth like they were in a contest to see who was the cleverest.

"What do the people at the paper say about dat storm?" Adrienne asked the General as she poured herself another mug of coffee. When she wasn't paying close attention to her words, she would substitute "dat" for "that."

"Haven't heard this morning, but it seems to be all in the Atlantic. I'm hoping it might even pull a high system in over us and bring us some less humid weather."

The General cleared the table. He had cooked the meal and was going to wash dishes. I had never seen my father do those things.

"You have carved out a real *aventure* for yourself," Adrienne said. "I hope you find what you're looking for."

"I just want to keep my p----romise to my friend."

Adrienne swung her legs up and over the bench seat. "I see my busboy is taking care of the dishes and I know you two men need to talk your river talk. I'll get a quick shower and be gone."

She walked over to my side of the table, rubbed some more powdered sugar off my nose and kissed me lightly on the cheek.

"Nice to be with you," Adrienne said. "And I'm here to say, I would trust you with any promise, sure."

Adrienne put the word "sure" at the end of a sentence like an exclamation mark. She went behind the bedroom curtain.

I went to the sink to help the General finish up with the dishes.

"I like the way Adrienne says her words," I said.

"She comes from an Acadian heritage. You probably know it as Cajun."

"She's really easy to talk to," I said.

"You'll find most of the folks in South Louisiana are like that," the General said, scrubbing his skillet. "I'm selfish. I wish I could wrap up this part of the country in a blanket and hide it. I'm afraid that television and the modern world will soon have us all talking and acting just alike and destroy all the different birthrights that make this country."

The General joked most of the time, but his serious side could take over without warning.

Adrienne stepped from behind the bedroom curtain with her hair pinned up. "*Tres bon*. I have both my men doing the dishes."

She stepped through the door to the bathroom. I heard the shower and then soft singing. I strained to hear the strange and exciting words.

Chapter 11

The General rolled out two large river charts on the table, holding down the corners with lead fishing weights and Adrienne's jar of flowers.

"Okay, all the womenfolk are gone, so let's get down to our river business." The General positioned his charts side-by-side on the table.

"C----an I ask something first? Is Adrienne your . . ."

Normally, I didn't want people to finish my sentences, but my question was personal and made me uncomfortable.

The General finished it for me. "My wife?"

I nodded.

"We're not legally married, but she's a long-time companion. We don't think too much about the future and make a lot of plans. Some people call New Orleans 'the Big Easy,' and we like to say that easy does it."

"I can tell you like to b----e with each other. Th----at's why I thought you might not be married."

"I sense a hidden editorial comment somewhere in there."

"I th----ink my mother and father don't like each other all that much. My father works late and travels all the time. I th----ink he works so much because he wants to get away from home."

The General sprinkled more sugar on the beignets and slid the plate over to me.

"I'm not a 'Dear Abby' kind of guy, but I was married once for a while and I know that wedded bliss is not always the smooth sail it seems like it should be."

The river charts I was so excited about were in front of us, but there I was, getting ready to empty out my problems to almost a stranger who wrote newspaper stories about hunting and fishing.

"I f----ound out that my father, who I really like a lot, is not my real father." There it was. The secret that nagged at me for the past six years was splashed out on top of the river charts.

"Have you talked to him about it?"

"I'm not g----ood at talking about that kind of stuff. And I'm not supposed to kn----ow about it anyway."

"Few of us are comfortable with conversations about those things," the General said. "But here's the rub. Not talking about something is the easy way out and in the end everything just starts to fester."

I had already emptied too much out on the General. The subject needed to be changed.

"I like Miss Adrienne." What I meant to say was that I liked the way she and the General talked to each other and enjoyed each other.

"Then I'd say you're a man of perception and good taste." The General moved the plate of beignets off the charts. "Now, let's get to the river—which, if I might add my own unsolicited comment—can be just as intriguing and mysterious as any woman."

The General explained in detail the two charts on the table in front of us. One was an Army Corps of Engineers channel chart that showed the Mississippi River from Baton Rouge to River Mile 0. The other was a U.S. Geological Survey chart of the lower delta as it fanned out with a bunch of skinny fingers toward the Gulf of Mexico.

"First, you have to understand that the Mississippi River flows at five hundred thousand cubic feet per second. Think of it as a fire hose that's a half mile wide."

The General talked about the river with the same excitement that Mr. Spiro talked about books and old philosophers.

"To the question of where the mouth might be located, you'll get different answers depending on the group of people you ask. The Corps of Engineers, the Coast Guard, the river pilot, and the commercial fisherman all have their own answers."

He pointed to River Mile 0 on the chart. "The Corps and the Coast Guard would say this is the mouth. The old-time river men would laugh at that."

"I d----idn't know it was going to be so complicated." I looked at the two charts filled with numbers and curved lines, much more detailed than my Esso road map. "Wonder why Mr. Spiro d----idn't give me more of a hint on where exactly to take him? He was b----orn in New Orleans and knew everything there was to know about the river."

"Maybe he wanted you to find it on your own." The General

looked away from the charts and straight at me. "Do you suppose his last request might actually have been for your benefit? A kind of parting gift."

A gift? The General's question spun in my head.

He let me stew and then continued his lesson. "When deep-sea fishermen go out for the first time, they unknowingly have in the back of their mind that there's going to be a big sign on a buoy that says 'Welcome to the Gulf Stream.'"

The mention of the Gulf Stream sent my mind wandering to the book in my gym bag. The General kept talking.

"The stream is real, but all it amounts to is a slight change in water temperature and maybe in color. Only the fish truly know where it is. The stream can move north or south as much as a hundred miles in a season."

"The old man kn----ew exactly where the Gulf Stream was when he caught his big fish." My sentence came out of left field, as my father liked to say.

"No doubt you're talking about Hemingway's Santiago."

I nodded. "It's my favorite b----ook in all the world. Have you read it?" I was excited to be thinking about the book again.

"Once or twice."

"Mr. Spiro said if you got right down to it, the b----ook is really about much more than just a man catching a big fish."

"As with most great books, it can be about anything you need it to be," the General said.

His comment and the fact he called it a great book sent my mind off on another wild-goose chase. I realized how much I had missed talking to Mr. Spiro about the book. The General gave me a moment before he took up his river lesson again.

"The river dumps so much sediment into the delta that its

mouth has to shift out of necessity. The Corps of Engineers can dredge a channel for ships, but it can't control the mouth," he said. "The Mississippi River spits out where it chooses."

"Y----ou're saying nobody can tell me for sure where the river becomes one with the sea, that p----lace that Mr. Spiro wanted me to find."

The General put his finger on the map.

"At Head of Passes, right where my finger is, the river splits into several smaller channels that make up what's called the birdfoot delta." He drew a big circle with his finger. "I would say the mouth is somewhere in this circle, but I would never presume to know its exact location."

I put my head in my hands and stared at the charts, expecting my confusion to cause the bad taste of bile to rise in my throat. The General poured himself another mug of coffee.

"I need to finish my column at the paper today, but I have an idea," he said. "I'm going to put you in contact with somebody who knows more about the Mississippi than all the so-called experts in Louisiana combined. If anybody can answer your question, he can. How does that sound?"

I swallowed hard.

"Good, good."

I finally felt satisfied that I was going to be meeting someone who could point me exactly where I needed to go on the river. Ever since I made my promise to Mr. Spiro, I wondered how I would feel if I let him down by not finding the true Mouth of the Mississippi River. I was getting closer now. I could feel it.

The General stepped behind the curtain to change clothes. I folded the sheets on the couch and packed my gym bag. Looking around the barge made me wonder if I would ever see it again.

In the middle of the table were the flowers that Adrienne had picked. Before Adrienne had left, she told me to be sure to take the rest of the beignets. I stuffed them in my gym bag.

My speech therapist once asked me if I stuttered more in front of people I knew well or if I stuttered more when I talked to strangers. I answered that I had trouble talking to strangers and getting to know them, seeing as how I felt extra pressure that I had to show them that there was nothing wrong with me. I had known Adrienne for only a few hours, but I already liked being around her and talking to her.

Chapter 12

The size of the bridge over the Mississippi River surprised me as the General drove back across to the newspaper side of the river. The bridge in New Orleans was twice as long as the bridge over the river in Memphis. I was so dead asleep in the General's truck the night before that I didn't realize we had crossed over such a steel monster. The water in the river didn't look like it was moving fast. It seemed almost flat, like Lake Pontchartrain, until you fixed your eyes on a floating log and looked back and forth from it to the bank. There was a good current, all right.

I had been saving up words for a question.

"Charlie t----old me the story of why you're called the General, but why do you call him Rocket?"

"I'm surprised that sobriquet didn't follow him to Memphis," the General said.

He set in telling me the story in his newspaper way.

Charlie had just been hired at the newspaper in Pine Bluff, Arkansas. He was working on the city desk one afternoon when a fire call came over the police scanner. Charlie recognized the address as the rooming house three blocks away, where he was staying. He ran out of the newspaper building at full speed.

The editor of the paper saw him racing out the front door and came by the city desk to ask where the new hire was going "like he was shot out of a rocket." Checking out a fire call, the city editor explained. Good to see such initiative in new employees, declared the editor, who pulled out a ten-dollar bill from his wallet and told the city editor to give it to Charlie when he got back.

Charlie returned to the newsroom later in the afternoon with his suitcase in one hand and his saxophone case in the other. From the pockets of his old raincoat, he pulled out a bottle of milk and a tabby kitten he had rescued from his apartment. Charlie put the kitten under his desk and poured it some milk in his coffee cup. The envelope on his desk with the ten-dollar bill in it was addressed to "Rocket Roker."

Ten bucks was a good day's wage at that time in Arkansas, the General assured me, and Charlie's nickname was forever cast in stone in the Little Rock newsroom.

★ ★ ★

The newspaper delivery trucks at the *Times-Picayune* were being refueled after the morning runs when we pulled in next to my car in the employee parking lot. I got out of the General's truck with my gym bag and sack of beignets.

The General said he was going into the newspaper building to have a switchboard operator place a long-distance call and that he would be right back. I unlocked the trunk to make certain Mr. Spiro's urn had made it safely through the night, put down the convertible top, and got out the Esso road map. I located the Mississippi River bridge that we had just crossed. The fiction of the road map once again matched the nonfiction of where I found myself.

The General returned with a piece of paper.

"I wish I had the day off to go down with you, but you'll be in good hands."

He handed me the piece of paper with a name, address, and a small hand-drawn map of Venice, Louisiana.

"Henri Moreau is the river man I told you about. He was already out on a charter when I called, but I talked to his wife. They'll be expecting you."

The simple change of the *y* to the French *i* turned "Henry" into *"On-ree"* with the accent on the second syllable. I liked the way the General pronounced it, but that didn't mean I could get it to come out of my mouth in that same way.

"Thanks for all your time and for setting me up with H----enry Moreau. Th----ink it's okay if I call him plain H----enry, 'cause I can't say it the way you do?"

"Not a problem," the General said. "You might want to just call him Captain. Everybody else does."

"T----ell Miss Adrienne goodbye for me."

"You bet. Now I want you to promise me something." The General gave me a stern look to let me know that he meant business. "On your way back through, I want you to give me a report on how you made out on the river. I checked with the newsroom and the U.S. Weather Service is keeping an eye on Hurricane Betsy even though it's way over in the Atlantic."

"I thought it was just a t----ropical storm."

"They upgraded it to a hurricane early this morning."

I had another thing to say to the General, but didn't know if I should. Why not? I was trying all types of new things.

"I like how you call me Son Vic."

"Old habit, giving people nicknames. Plus, Charlie told me I was to treat you like you were my son."

"I used to give friends n----icknames, too."

The General nodded.

"But m----ost of the time it was because I couldn't say their real names." I was blabbering but I had to keep going. "I also used to be afraid of putting c----ommas in my writing, but I learned from Mr. Spiro that commas are just another part of life you had to deal with."

Words spilled out of me without making much sense. I realized I didn't want to say goodbye to the General.

"Your Mr. Spiro was a wise friend," the General said. "Remember now, give me a shout on the way back." He pushed my door closed.

I had known Ray Patton for not even a full day, but waving goodbye was hard. There's no way he could have understood what I meant by being afraid of commas or how much it bothered me that my father was not my birth father, but maybe friends, even 24-hour friends, could have good conversations without having to do a lot of explaining.

I headed out of the parking lot and south back across the bridge. The typewriter on the floorboard seemed out of place again. I still didn't have a good answer why I thought I had to bring it, but there it was. Going with me to meet the man who finally could tell me where to find the Mouth of the Mississippi River for Mr. Spiro.

My promise seemed simple at first. Find the end of the river, the mouth. Spread the ashes. But the closer I got, the more complicated everything was getting. Mr. Spiro had never let me down and I was not going to let him down. He spent hours and hours answering my questions and teaching me all that I didn't understand about myself. When Mr. Spiro went away, a big hole started following me around, and the only way to close it was to put his ashes exactly where they belonged. I didn't have much time to do it, either, before I had to get back to Memphis and start my job. And college.

Chapter 13

The General had given me directions out of the city to State Highway 23, which would take me to Venice, 75 miles south of New Orleans and the last town on the Mississippi River accessible by road. He explained that I was going into a part of Louisiana that maybe was different than any other place in the world. The farther south I went, he explained, it would be more and more difficult to distinguish the river from the Gulf of Mexico.

Captain Henri Moreau lived in Venice and, according to the General, was a long-time river pilot whose job was to board ocean-going ships and guide them upriver to New Orleans and Baton Rouge. He had retired from that job and now was much in demand as a deep-sea fishing guide on his charter boat.

The names of the small towns on Highway 23 sounded even more exotic than the Mississippi towns from the day before. Jesuit Bend. Pointe a la Hache. Triumph. Bohemia. Port Sulphur.

A new language surrounded me as I followed the river south through this part of Louisiana. Small cafés at the side of the highway advertised jambalaya and *étouffée*. Names on signs ended with the mystery of the silent *x*. Boudreaux. Babineaux. Robicheaux. Fonteneaux.

Having to learn a foreign language was one of the things worrying me about going to college. My advisor already had warned me that if I didn't take a foreign language my freshman year, it would be mandatory as a sophomore. How was I going to learn to speak a foreign language when I was having so much trouble speaking my own?

The air on Highway 23 was much like the thick air crossing Lake Pontchartrain. Memphis was humid enough in late summer, but the humidity in South Louisiana was another kind that covered you like a heavy blanket. The air conditioning would have been going full blast in my parents' cars.

The tiny town of Happy Jack had one service station with a single pump. The attendant, unlike Fred in Mississippi, didn't wear a uniform. Blotches of grease covered his undershirt.

"How far to . . . to the town . . . town of Venice?" I had to sneak up on the *v* sound carefully.

"Thirty minutes," the attendant said, except he pronounced it "tirty" with a silent *h*.

"Do I keep on this highway?"

"Rat down dat way, sure."

"How's the fishing?" I asked, not that I was the least bit interested in fishing. I wanted to hear more of the language that made ordinary words sound like a new kind of poetry.

"Yellow fin been bite *tres bon*."

"What are they b----iting?" I hoped the question sounded legitimate.

"Been lovin' dem shiny jig wid skirt running up top, hear told."

"Okay. Thanks for the info."

"*Bonne journée.*"

I pulled away from the pump. All spoken language was foreign to me, some just more foreign than others. But I liked this new one I was hearing.

★ ★ ★

Green road signs the full length of Highway 23 declared it the "Official Evacuation Route." Not only was it official, according to my Esso map, it was the only way in and the only way out. The river was on both sides of the road that cut through a narrow spit of land. Or was it the Gulf of Mexico now on both sides of the road? The General was right. I couldn't tell.

A larger sign greeted me: "Venice, Louisiana—Fishing Capital of the World."

I drove slowly as more traffic filled the highway. Almost every building in town sat high on stilts. The main floors of houses and businesses served as shelters for cars, trucks, and all manner of small boats. The space under the houses also contained, more often than not, outboard motors attached to saw horses, rows of gasoline cans, and rusty tanks of propane.

The Moreau home was on Jump Basin Road between the highway and the river. I followed the General's hand-drawn map to a house of dull-gray weathered wood that was the largest one on the street, sitting about the width of a football field from the riverbank. Stairways on both ends led up to a porch that wrapped all the way around the house. Guy-wires anchored a tall antenna on the roof. A rusty pickup truck sat on the concrete pad under the house. Wooden picnic tables and odds and ends of fishing equipment covered the rest of the house's foundation. Two barefoot girls sat on an old wooden boat overturned near the river. The older girl sang while she braided the younger one's dark hair.

I parked on crushed shells at what I took to be the front of the house and climbed the long flight of stairs. A woman wiping her hands on her apron greeted me through the screen door.

"You dat Memphis boy name of Vic that the General called about?" she said with a big smile.

"Y----es, mam. I guess I found the right house."

"I guess you rightly did. My name's Genevieve Moreau. Gene for short. Henri's my husband you came down to see. Come on in." She said Henri the same way that the General did. The way I couldn't.

Her accent was not as heavy as the gas station attendant's, but there was no doubt she had the heritage of South Louisiana. A large table, again with bench seats, dominated the open room I walked into. On three sides, screened windows served as the top portion of the walls. Kitchen cabinets stretched all the way down one side of the room. An attic fan like the one in our old house in Memphis gently shook the house, perched on its tall legs. An assortment of chairs and worn couches filled other parts of the room. A tiny television sat on a desk along with a shortwave radio similar to the one at the newspaper.

"Thought you might bring the General with you," Mrs. Moreau said.

"He had to work."

She offered a quick laugh. "That's a good 'un. The General likes to say he can't even spell 'work.' Take a seat and I'll get you a cold NuGrape if them kids left any."

An athletic-looking woman in a purple dress, Mrs. Moreau

appeared to be about the same age as my mother, but in much better shape, like she did a lot of physical outside work. She wiped the bottle of grape soda on her apron and handed it to me.

"Let me try to raise Henri and see how far out he is," Mrs. Moreau said, before leaning over the desk and flipping switches on the radio. She clicked the button twice on the hand mic attached to the radio by a squiggly cord.

"She-Gene to *Rooster Tale*. Come in. Over."

She spun a knob to a different frequency and clicked twice again.

"She-Gene to the *Rooster*. Do you read me?"

"*Rooster* to She-Gene. Over."

"What's your ETA? Over."

"Fifteen hundred hours. Over."

"See you low. Over."

Mrs. Moreau returned the mic to its hook.

"Did you understand any of that jib-jabber?"

I shook my head.

"Henri says he'll be in at three o'clock. The *Rooster Tale* is his charter boat. My radio name is She-Gene since my brother is also named Gene. He goes by 'He-Gene' so they can tell us apart on the radio. Clear as mud, huh?"

"What d----oes 'see you low' mean?"

"It's an old shrimpers' saying. A boat riding low in the water means it's full of fresh catch. It now just means something like 'see you when you get here.'"

Another language for me to learn.

I checked my wristwatch. It would be more than five hours until I could talk with Captain Henri Moreau, but there was nothing I could do about it. I had hoped to take care of my promise to Mr. Spiro and start back home, but I was depending on other people now. I thought again about what I was putting my mother and father through, but I erased it from my thinking as quickly as I could.

She-Gene busied herself in the kitchen while she told me more about her family. She and the Captain had five children—three girls, two boys. Her brother, He-Gene, lived downriver in a place called Pilottown where he was in charge of a station that supplied river pilots to ocean freighters coming into ports at New Orleans and Baton Rouge. All freighters, she explained, had to take a licensed river pilot on board to go anywhere above Pilottown. Her husband had been a pilot for 25 years before he retired and bought the *Rooster Tale.*

"Got his river license at twenty-two," She-Gene said. "Youngest pilot ever on the river, sure. And the best."

She-Gene opened the refrigerator and looked through its contents. "Did you meet Adrienne at the General's place?"

"Y----es, ma'am. I liked her."

"Even though she's a far-cousin to me, I'll have to say she's some kind of good for the General. She knows just how much line to let out on him. I think they make a good *paire.*"

She-Gene pulled out all sizes of pots and pans from underneath the kitchen counter, talking all the while.

"Wish Adrienne was down here now to help me with this cooking for tonight. If that old storm will stay over in the Atlantic, we're having us a *fais do-do.*"

"What's a 'f----ay doe-doe?'" The *f* sound was normally easy for me as it let out its own air, but when I couldn't see a word in my head, it was harder to start the sound without a stutter.

"You'll find out soon enough. We usually don't do a *fais do-do* on a Tuesday night, but my Henri turns fifty today. You're invited, sure."

I didn't know how to tell this nice woman I had just met that I didn't have time to be going to a birthday party and that I needed to get back home as soon as possible to explain to my parents where I had been.

A radio on the kitchen counter played softly as She-Gene busied herself at the stove with her pots and pans. I looked around the room to see if there might be a picture of Captain Henri Moreau somewhere. I already had a sense in my head of what the river captain might look like and I wanted to see if they matched, but there was nothing on the walls except for a river chart.

Over the living room mantle in our house in Memphis was a painting of my mother and father that was done on one of their trips to New Orleans. I never liked the way my mother's eyes would follow me from the painting anytime I walked through the room.

"D----o you . . . H----ave you ever heard the Captain talk about how to find the mouth of the river?"

"The river, the gulf, the tide, the fish . . . that's all they talk about down here, but I can't say I've heard any talk about the mouth. The General says that's what you're down here looking for."

I nodded.

"Best thing I can tell you is that if there's a mouth to be found, Henri Moreau is the one who can find it for you, sure."

Chapter 14

A steaming mound of boiled shrimp covered the newspaper spread out in front of me.

The attic fan and the breeze coming off the river made the Moreau house comfortable in the South Louisiana heat, even with the eyes on the gas stove going full blast.

She-Gene had asked if I knew how to peel boiled shrimp. I said I did but soon found out that I didn't.

She showed me how to snap off the head and legs, pop the meat out of the shell and use my fingernail to scrape off the black vein on the back of the shrimp that she explained was its digestive tract.

"You're getting it now," She-Gene said. "I don't put no shrimp in my jambalaya that's not been veined, sure." She sounded like Adrienne with the way she used "sure" as a punctuation mark.

The yappy noise of a small motorbike came to a stop

underneath the house and then footsteps of someone taking the stairs two at a time.

"Momma, who dat sporty car belong to?" a dark-haired girl asked as she flung open the screen door.

Her hair was short, but not short enough to discourage the head full of wayward curls. She wore a faded-green waitress uniform that anybody could see was too large for her. She took off the belt that had bunched up the uniform around her waist. She looked at me, flakes of shrimp shells covering the front of my shirt. I looked at her, barefoot and holding her white canvas shoes in one hand.

"This is Vic, come down from Memphis," She-Gene said. "The General sent him down to talk with your daddy about going out on the river."

Shrimp shells fluttered to the floor when I stood.

"Phil is our oldest," She-Gene said. "Philomene is her given name, but she goes mostly by 'Phil.'"

"That sporty car must belong to you," the girl said.

I nodded.

Philomene Moreau walked to the table, picked a peeled shrimp out of the bowl in front of me and plopped it in her mouth.

"You best vein them shrimp good, Sporty Boy," she said. "Momma don't 'low no dirty shrimp in her gumbo."

She crossed the room and headed down the back hall before I could come up with anything to say.

"Phil waitresses some at Maison's down by the marina. She'd rather be out on the *Rooster* but her daddy won't pay her nothing. You'll see she can be something else, sure."

Something else is exactly what she was. She moved like a

shortstop but was as pretty as any cheerleader. Her dark eyes drilled into me when she looked at me. Her tan was not the swimming pool kind that disappeared a week after school started.

"H----ow old is your d----aughter?" I pretended still to be interested in the pile of shrimp in front of me.

"Eighteen, soon be nineteen. Been out of school for a year or so. We thought she might go on with her schooling, but she'd rather work on the boat even if her daddy won't pay her nothin'."

"I'm starting c----ollege next week, but some of my friends are taking a year off before they start." I felt the urge to make an excuse for the girl named Phil even though I had just met her.

"Never seen a girl so crazy about boats. She's not happy unless she's on the river or out in the gulf."

The pile of peeled and veined shrimp in the bowl grew larger. At first my thoughts while peeling had been on taking care of my promise and getting back to Memphis as soon as possible, but I couldn't get my mind off the barefooted girl who had exploded into the house.

As fast as she had disappeared down the hall, the girl returned in quick strides across the room and over to the shortwave radio. The waitress uniform was gone, replaced by cutoff jeans and a faded red-plaid shirt with the sleeves rolled up above her elbows. The jeans shorts were not the knee-length or even mid-thigh shorts that girls in Memphis wore. This girl wore the shortest of shorts. We learned about adjective case in sophomore English— short, shorter, shortest. These shorts were not comparative. They were superlative.

The girl clicked the hand mic twice.

"Phil to *Rooster*. Come in."

"*Rooster* here. Over."

"Say ETA," she said in that quick, snappy radio voice that I envied. "Over."

"I jes' told your momma. Over."

"So . . . told your daughter, too. Over."

"Fifteen hundred hours. Over."

"See you low. Out."

Phil joined her mother at the kitchen counter. Concentrating on the pile of shrimp in front of me grew even more difficult. The mother and daughter chatted about seasonings and cooking times as they tasted and tended to the pots that simmered on the stove.

The radio clicked twice.

"*Crazy Eights* to Phil. Come in."

Again.

"*Crazy Eights* to Phil. You off work yet? How 'bout you come out and play?"

"You'd better answer that Jimmy or he'll pester you till sundown," She-Gene said, stirring a big pot.

Phil threw her dishrag on the counter, stomped over to the radio, and grabbed the hand mic. Her dark eyes—eyes like Adrienne's—opened wide.

"You go on out and play with yourself, Jimmy LaBue. Over and out."

The radio made a high-pitched squeal as she switched it off.

"Philomene, shush that kind of talk. You know better than to be like that on the radio," She-Gene said. "And mind you, we got company in the house."

Phil walked back to the kitchen counter.

"I'm tired of that no-good *couyon* bothering me. He's up to nothing but bad, sure, in dat hot-rod boat of his." I heard her deep accent for the first time.

The mother and daughter continued the conversation that sounded more like sisters talking. They occasionally slipped into a string of French or Cajun words. I could eavesdrop only in English.

I took the full bowl of peeled shrimp to She-Gene at the sink.

"A----nything else I can do until the Captain gets here?"

"Didn't mean to work your fingers to the bone," She-Gene said. "Phil, cut a lemon for Vic and let him wash his hands."

Phil took a lemon from a hanging wire basket and sliced it in half. "Hold your palms over the sink," she instructed. She squeezed every drop from the lemon halves. My hands were full of pulp.

She-Gene pulled out a clean hand towel from a drawer.

"Phil, why don't you take Vic and go find the kids and tell them they got to get early baths tonight for the party. And remind them that they got to register for school tomorrow."

Phil handed me a bar of Ivory soap. "Finish washing with this, Sporty Boy. I don't want no shrimp stink round me."

"Stop talking like that, Phil," She-Gene said. "Vic's a guest in our house and he don't know how you are. Try to behave yourself for once."

Phil winked at me.

"He's a big city boy, Momma. He knows I'm just messin' with him."

I dried my hands and followed my barefoot host in her short-shorts through the front door and down the long flight of stairs. Without a doubt. Superlative case.

As I had explained in my clumsy way to Adrienne that morning on the barge, talking with girls my own age was difficult for me. What did they think of my stutter? Did it make me seem like a weirdo in their eyes?

A date with a girl was something I dreaded. The conversations always ended up sounding phony with the way I skipped around words and sounds. Going to a movie and to a drive-in restaurant afterward was more exhausting for me than running wind sprints after baseball practice.

I discovered as we walked along the river that talking with Phil was different. My hesitations and prolongations didn't seem to matter to her. Her eyes never drifted when she looked at me and they seemed to be telling me that she wasn't concerned about the way I talked.

We found her two younger sisters playing in a pile of old fishing nets by the river. It was the same girls I had seen on the overturned boat. They were busy weaving cattail stalks into the nets.

"You two better get all your playing out of you," Phil said. "Momma's taking you to school tomorrow to register."

They looked up at their big sister from their handiwork.

"And remember that tonight is Daddy's *fais do-do*. You get home in time for baths, you hear what I'm a told you?"

The sisters nodded and returned to their playful weaving.

"Them two girls could spend all day foolin' with an old shrimp net," Phil said.

We walked on past smaller houses farther from the river. She found her two brothers outside a small market, rinsing and stacking empty bottles of Dixie Beer into wooden crates. Phil gave them the same orders for early baths. The older one explained that yesterday's Labor Day crowd had given them a load of bottles to clean and sort and they were making good money from the owner of the market.

"If you don't be home in time for baths, Momma will blame me and you'll have me on you like white on rice."

"I know'd dat," the older brother said. "Don't worry yourself."

He looked me over. "Who dat?"

"This is Vic, down here to talk 'bout going out with Daddy on the *Rooster*. You'll see his little car at the house and you two don't be bothering it."

"They r----eally can't hurt anything," I said.

"You don't know these two rapscallions. They might have the engine out of it and in a boat by the time we get back." The brothers resumed rinsing and stacking bottles.

We walked along the river's edge again. Phil asked questions about what my life was like in Memphis, and I answered without feeling much of a need to search for good starter sounds.

"Seems to me like you spend as much time playing baseball as I do on the river," she said. "Are you any good?"

"The c----oach at Southwestern says I have a good arm . . . but I decided just before I came down here that I'm not going to play."

"Why not?"

"I want to work p----art-time at the newspaper and I can't do both. I have to k----eep my grades up 'cause of V---- . . . 'cause of the war in Southeast Asia."

"If you're so good at baseball, seems like you're missing out by not playing."

"It's hard to explain. I just feel like being around the p----eople at the newspaper is b----etter than playing on a baseball team."

Phil shrugged her shoulders. *"C'est la vie."*

"What does that mean?"

"That's life. Whatever makes you happy, pappy."

Phil picked up two bleached shells about the same size from the riverbank. She handed me one.

"You'd better out chuck me or I'm not believing this business about your baseball," she said.

She slung the shell far out into the river with a sidearm move that didn't fit my idea of how a girl was supposed to throw. I followed with my own sidearm throw that to my surprise only outdistanced hers by a few feet.

"Okay, Sporty Boy. I believe your baseball story now." She smiled. "You don't mind me testing you, do you?"

I shook my head. I didn't mind anything that Philomene Moreau did.

★ ★ ★

Since my final conversation with Mr. Spiro in the hospital, the prospect of reaching the Mouth of the Mississippi River had taken over most of my free-time thinking. Phil had interrupted those thoughts when she exploded through the screen door. As difficult as it was in the presence of Phil, I made myself focus again on what brought me all the way to Venice, Louisiana.

"Have you ever seen the Mouth of the Mississippi River?"

"Have you ever seen the end of a rainbow?" Phil shot back.

"I'm serious. I told a friend I would find the mouth of the river for him and I'm going to keep my p----romise one way or another." My words came out aggressive. The tone was unlike me, but Phil took up the challenge.

"You don't think I'm serious, Sporty Boy?" Her eyes dug into me. "You hear what I'm telling you. The river is real, so it must have a beginning and an end. A rainbow is real and somewhere it has to have an end, but that don't mean that finding either one is a *garanti*."

Phil used her French accent for emphasis the way I used my fastball on a first pitch to get a batter's attention.

"Sorry. I just m----eant that finding the mouth of the river is important to me. I made a special p----romise to my friend before he . . . when he was in the hospital."

Phil grabbed my hand and held it tight. "Come on then, Sporty Boy. Let's go sit on the dock and you can tell me all about your friend and your *promesse*."

Holding hands with girls at the movies or while walking down the midway at the Mid-South Fair was almost as hard as talking to them. Girls' hands were soft and my hands were rough with calluses and only good at gripping a baseball or grinding the handle of a bat. Phil's hands were different, rough as mine and just as strong. She didn't let go of her grip until we were seated on the dock with our feet dangling above the river.

I found myself telling Phil everything about Mr. Spiro, starting with the day I first met him and how I blacked out on his front porch trying to tell him my name. I had never told anyone that story. Not even Mam. I took out my billfold and showed Phil my taped-together dollar bill.

"Each week I collected for the paper from Mr. Spiro, he would give me a corner of a dollar bill with a word written on it."

"What do those words have to do with one another?"

"He called it the 'Quartering of the Soul,' and I'm still working on what they mean . . . but I think I have an idea. It has something to do with the best way to divide up yourself to make sure you're living the best life you can."

I told her about the urn in my car and the promise I had made.

"So, why did you like your Mr. Spiro so much?"

No one had ever asked me that question. The answer seemed obvious, but I still had to hunt for the right words to explain it.

"You know how you underline sentences when you're studying something for school b----ecause you think what you just read is important?"

Phil nodded.

"Well, when I talked with Mr. Spiro it was like I wanted to underline everything he said."

Phil's eyes and the way she asked real questions—not questions just to be nice or to keep the conversation going—made me want to tell her everything that was inside of me. And I did. About my struggles with my speech. About how my lack of self-confidence with the way I talked made people, especially my parents, want to protect me more than I thought was good for somebody my age. I told her how upset my parents were going to be with me when I got back to Memphis.

"Seems to me you don't lack much for confidence if you want to go out and tangle with the Mississippi River."

"It's just something I have to do. For Mr. Spiro . . . and m----aybe for myself."

I had never shared my secret thoughts to anyone like I had

done with Phil. Certainly not a stranger. Certainly not a girl who was just a year older than me.

In turn, I decided I wanted to know everything about Philomene Moreau, but she did not gush with information like I did.

"Living down here on the river suits me. That's all," she said. "I even enjoy foolin' with my little brothers and sisters and giving them a hard time."

"Your mother said you like g----oing out on the boat with your father."

"You bet I do."

"What about college?"

"What about it?"

"Are you thinking about g----oing anytime soon?"

Phil's expression told me I wasn't going to get an answer to my question. She looked down at the river.

"Did Momma put you up to asking me that?"

"No. I just mentioned to her I would be starting when I got b----ack home and she said they thought you might be thinking about c----ollege . . . at some point."

Phil continued to stare down at the river while she composed an answer that I suspected would be the end of this part of the conversation.

"Let's just say I don't do much thinking on it," she said.

The surface of the water looked calm enough, but underneath the river was rushing with its fire-hose energy to the Gulf of Mexico. I could only believe that the same thing was going on inside Philomene Moreau from Venice, Louisiana.

Chapter 15

My extended walk along the river with Phil made me wonder if traveling to new places opened up a person's mind with new ways of thinking about things. My head had always been full of thoughts of baseball and copying words on my typewriter. New thoughts bombarded me now like stinging raindrops after getting caught with my convertible top down.

"I've t----alked so much my mouth is dry," I said. "Could I get a drink of water at your house?"

"For someone who says he has trouble talking to people, you can sure get on with it," Phil said. Her smile and wink turned what might have seemed like a criticism into a compliment.

I never seemed to be that comfortable visiting the houses where my friends lived, but I was happy to see the Moreau house again on its tall stilt legs. Phil opened a rusted refrigerator under the house and took out a NuGrape. She took a long swig, wiped off the top of the bottle with her palm, and handed it to me. We sat on top of one of the picnic tables. Phil brushed off the soles of her feet, which appeared to have the texture of an old catcher's mitt left out in the rain.

"How can you walk on c----rushed shells and gravel without any shoes?" I liked to go barefoot on the beach, but that was about it.

"Been doing it going on nineteen years. Do anything long enough and you get to where it don't bother you none."

"N----ot stuttering," I said.

I thought my bold response would throw her off and get us back to where we were before I asked her about going to college. She didn't flinch.

"Why you worry so much 'bout how you talk? You in Sout' Louisiana where all a body talk funny, sure." She could turn her accent on and off for emphasis. "I don't hear you stutter anyhow, so much as you just kind of sputter sometimes."

All my life I had considered myself a person who stuttered and now I was informed that all I did was "sputter," like an engine that was only in need of a little fine tuning. A sputter was better than a stutter in my book.

She jumped down from the table, her bare feet crunching the shells and gravel. She grabbed my left wrist and twisted it to look at my watch.

"Let's take that little sporty car of yours over to the marina. The *Rooster* should be coming in soon." Phil changed her mood and the subject of conversations like the wind changed directions.

I had forgotten about my typewriter on the passenger-side floorboard.

"Let me put that on a table under the house," I said, but she had already slid into the car with her knees pulled up and her feet resting on the front of the bucket seat.

"It's not far. What do you do with this thing anyway?"

"I type on it—I c----opy stuff—when I probably should be doing other things."

The incomplete answer seemed to satisfy the girl, who surely had the toughest feet in South Louisiana.

* * *

The traffic on Highway 23 was mostly pickup trucks hauling boat trailers. Some of the trailers were twice as long as the trucks pulling them. My father had a summer cabin on Moon Lake in Mississippi that he kept mainly for the people in his office and their families. We didn't use it often since I had so many baseball games in the summer, and my mother said the place was "a little on the crude side," but I liked to go down and haul the ski boat in and out of the water with a truck that stayed at the cabin. Against my mother's wishes, my father taught me to drive the truck and back the boat trailer long before I got my driver's license. I remembered those times as some of the best I ever had with my father. It was nice to be alone with him and have him teach me how to do things in his calm way.

"What size is your father's charter boat?" I asked. Phil had gone quiet on me, but I figured she would like talking about the *Rooster Tale*.

"Thirty-seven feet." She answered without taking her eyes off the passenger-side rearview mirror.

I asked Phil where the boat got its name. No answer. She leaned forward against her knees, staring at the mirror. A red truck with oversized tires swerved to pass a car behind us and came close up on our tail, almost touching my bumper. She turned around in her seat and looked at the truck.

"I knew it. That *couyon* is following us," Phil said, tightening her arms around her knees.

"Who?"

"Jimmy LaBue from over in Cutoff. The one on the marine radio. I can't make that Cajun stop sniffing round me."

"What's that name you called him?"

"*Couyon*. Crazy in the head."

Phil told me where to park in the marina's paved lot. She jumped out of the car before it came to a full stop, slamming the door and running over to the truck when it pulled in near us.

"I told you not to be coming round me, Spy Boy," Phil said to the driver in the cab.

The door of the shiny Chevrolet Apache opened. The pickup truck had amber lights on its roof like the tractor-trailer rigs on the highway. The rear-view mirrors stuck out like silver wings. The windows were heavily tinted.

"Just wantin' to meet dat new friend of yours, *cherie*," Jimmy LaBue said in an accent much heavier than Phil's.

He wore black jeans with a sleeveless shirt tightly tucked in, and red cowboy boots with silver tips on the toes. On his belt was a fish-filleting knife in a long leather sheath. My mother had a similar knife in the set she bought for her new kitchen. The knife took on a more threatening look hanging on a belt.

LaBue walked past Phil without looking at her and up to me. He stuck out his hand. He had tattoos on the inside of both forearms, which didn't have much meat on them, making his blue veins stand out like lines on a roadmap.

"James LaBue here. Welcome to Sout' Louisiana."

Phil moved in between us before I could shake his hand.

"Reckon you drove all the way down here from Tennessee in dat little t'ing just to see us?" He motioned with his head to my car without taking his eyes off me.

"This is Vic," Phil said. "He's down from Memphis to go out on the *Rooster*. My daddy's gonna be coming in just any minute now. We got to go meet him."

LaBue ignored Phil. He glanced down at my feet.

"Don't college boys wear them kind of leather shoes now without no socks? You must be one of them college boys."

"Starting soon." I was glad for the two s-words in a row. I concentrated on maintaining good eye contact. LaBue was a couple of inches taller, but I was stockier. He moved closer.

"So, what you going out fishing for, college boy?"

I didn't want to get into the fact that I wasn't interested in fishing and didn't know anything about it, but then recalled my conversation that morning at the service station in Happy Jack.

"Y----ellowfins. H----ear they're b----iting well."

The *y* sound was never a good starter sound for a sentence. I had to stretch it out or it would cause a hard block. I added the extra sentence to try to cover up the bad start but could get the extra words out only by taking some hard breaths and slurring my sounds. My stuttering usually went downhill fast during a challenge and there was no doubt that Jimmy LaBue had a challenge on his mind.

"What you gonna use on them y----ellowf----ins?" He mocked my stutter by drawing out the sound a lot more than I did.

"Shiny j----igs with skirt. T----op up."

The *s* sound came out okay but I had to slur and draw out the *j* sound to get through the block and I wasn't sure what the service station attendant had meant by "up top," so those words got reversed. Trying to fool somebody when I didn't know what I was talking about was another skill I lacked. I had gotten lucky on coming up with an answer on Jimmy LaBue's fishing question, but my stuttering had put itself on parade. And maybe the worst thing I did was lose eye contact when my eyes dropped down to his red cowboy boots. I saw they were made out of alligator hide.

"We got to meet the *Rooster* now," Phil said. She pulled me by the arm.

LaBue looked at her for the first time. "Why you fooling with this *bégayer* boy, *cherie?*"

"*Je te préviens.* Leave us be, Jimmy." Phil pulled me toward the marina docks.

"Where you come off warning me, bitch?" LaBue said.

She didn't look back as we walked toward the marina.

The truck's tires screeched on the blacktop of the parking lot. Phil didn't let go of my arm until we reached the boat slips.

"I never figured you for a sport fisherman." Some of the tension had left her voice. "So, just what exactly do you know about yellowfin tuna?"

"N----ot much. I didn't even know a y----ellowfin was a tuna." I told her about my conversation at the filling station in Happy Jack.

She squeezed my arm and laughed, but I got serious.

"W----hat was that name he called me?"

"Nothing. Forget it."

"It started with a *b.*"

"Forget it, I'm telling you. It's nothing."

I let it drop, but there was no way I was going to forget it. I could tell by its context exactly what it meant. I wasn't good at saying words, but I was hard to beat when it came to understanding them.

* * *

The *Rooster Tale* was impressive with its sleek hull and tall extension on top of the cabin that had a duplicate set of controls. The boat eased into its large slip. Phil leaped aboard.

I watched her work from a bench on the wharf. She grabbed the heavy lines, tied quick knots, and heaved the lines to the dock. She hopped off the boat with a line in hand and made a figure eight with it around a dock cleat, wrapping it under itself on the last turn and then jerking it snug.

She shoved a gangplank from the dock onto the boat as Captain Henri Moreau backed down the flybridge ladder. Phil gave her father a hug. He had on khaki shorts like the ones I wore. His thick arms and legs were dark from the sun. The ball cap pulled down over his eyes was stained and ragged. Sunglasses hung from a cord around his neck. He didn't look anything like I had imagined him. He was not much taller than I was, but if I were pitching to him, I certainly wouldn't give him a good ball to hit. He looked like he could knock anything out of the park.

The *Rooster*'s three charter customers for the day, all on the chubby side with white sunblock slathered on their faces, stepped off the boat. Phil steadied them and their wobbly legs on the gangplank.

"How'd it go out there, fellas?" Phil asked.

"Pretty good," said the one with the biggest belly. "See what the Captain thinks."

Captain Moreau took inventory at the large ice chest that ran the length of the stern.

"Two nice yellowfins, a bunch of snapper, some nice grouper."

"Not too bad for a bunch of old guys." Phil's wink cushioned her words. She could get by with saying anything to anybody with her wink and smile.

Captain Moreau began slinging the smaller fish one by one onto the dock. Phil put on a pair of cloth gloves and grabbed a fish in each hand by sticking her thumb in the mouths. She hooked them under their gills on metal spikes below a *"Rooster Tale* for Charter" sign.

"C----an I help?" I asked.

"I might need some help with those yellowfins you know so much about." She winked at me.

"Too big to hang," Captain Moreau said to his daughter. "See if the guys want their picture taken. I think one of them went to get a camera."

Phil gathered the three men underneath the sign and instructed them on how to hold one of the big tunas in front of them.

"Now everybody smile and say *'Rooster,'*" Phil said.

"I'll make sure everything is iced after I scrub down here," Captain Moreau said to the three men. He jumped onto the dock to uncoil a water hose. Phil waved me over.

"This is Vic, the General's friend from Memphis. He wants to talk with you about going out on the river."

Captain Moreau stuck out his hand that felt like it might have even tougher skin than the bottom of Phil's feet.

"Good to meet you, son. My wife radioed me after the General called this morning. I'll be glad to try to help if I can."

Phil uncoiled the rest of the hose for her father.

"You remember your party tonight, don't you, Daddy?"

"I don't know why we're having it, much less on a Tuesday night," the Captain said.

"Momma wanted to have it before school started, and, after all, today *is* your birthday."

"I'll be on home after I get the *Rooster* scrubbed and the catch iced down." Captain Moreau turned to me. "We can talk tonight about exactly what you're looking for."

"If you don't need me, Daddy, I'm going to show Vic around Venice some."

"Afraid there's not much to see here," Captain Moreau said.

"I like it here, sir. All this is n----ew to me."

"See you at the house, then." The captain turned on the water and began washing down the *Rooster Tale*.

Phil scanned the marina parking lot in all directions as we walked back to my car. The concern on her face had turned into an excited twinkle in her eyes by the time she opened the car door.

"I have a secret spot for us to go if you're up for it," she said. "I bet you're gonna like it."

If the spot included Phil, I would like it. Earlier in the day I had hoped there would be enough time in the afternoon for Captain Moreau to take me out on the river and to my destination. I could finish my business and be back on the road home before the end of the day. After spending most of the afternoon with Philomene Moreau, I wasn't in such a hurry anymore.

Chapter 16

Phil directed me around the bayous, canals, and bridges that chopped up the lower sliver of Louisiana on which Venice was located. My passenger's odd posture caused by my out-of-place typewriter had begun to seem normal. Not only could she tie knots, she could tie herself in a knot and still look comfortable.

Unlike my few dates in Memphis who appeared to be concerned mainly about their hairdos when riding in my car with the top down, Phil never fussed with her hair or even so much as touched it. The only phrase I remembered from world history class was *laissez faire*, which was French for letting things take their natural course. That was Phil all the way. I wanted to look at her instead of the narrow roads that wound through the fields and swamps.

"Take that dirt road up there to the right. I'll jump out and get the gate."

She unhooked a chain wrapped around a fence post and waved me through. There was a gate, all right, but that was it. No fence on either side.

I expected Phil to settle back in the car, but she took off running in her bare feet through the knee-high grass that covered the flat land as far as I could see.

"Follow me," she shouted.

She had me park at a dilapidated building with a rusted-through tin roof and pieces of its walls missing.

"Come on, Sporty Boy. See if you can catch you a swampy."

I got out of the car and followed Phil into the field, unclear of exactly what she had called on me to do.

"What's a swampy?"

"A swamp rabbit. First to catch one gets a prize."

I struggled to keep up with Phil as she zigzagged through the tall grass, still not certain what we were up to.

"Go find your own swampy," she said. "This is my *territoire.*" With her accent, Phil could turn a plain vanilla word into a chocolate sundae.

She was serious about catching a swamp rabbit, I decided, instead of running for the sake of running. Penny loafers with slick leather soles weren't the best for meeting a Jimmy LaBue or chasing rabbits, but I gave it everything I had.

"Here, rabbit. Here, little rabbit," I called out as I ran in circles and flapped my arms.

When I turned, Phil had her hands on her knees.

"Are you okay?"

She raised her head, but was laughing so hard she had trouble getting her breath. She took off again across the field, flattening the tall grass and stirring up dry clouds of seeds and husks.

"There's a buck," Phil shouted. "Circle round and run it over here."

Ahead of me, an animal in full stride popped up above the grass. The rabbit was twice the size of the white bunnies in the Easter displays at Goldsmith's department store in Memphis. With its long ears and legs, the animal looked more like a kangaroo than a rabbit.

"Don't run to where it just landed," Phil instructed. "You got to lead it some."

If Phil wanted to catch a rabbit, no matter how unlikely it might seem, that's what I wanted. I took up the chase all out. We stayed on the rabbit's trail and then Phil, anticipating the rabbit's next jump, launched herself in midair in a perfectly timed leap. She grabbed the rabbit's hind legs before both she and the animal hit the ground. The rabbit jerked out of her grip and bounded off through the grass. I gave chase only to see it jump into a bayou and swim away.

"It's swimming," I shouted. "That crazy r----abbit is swimming."

I looked back to see Phil on the ground and not moving. I hurried to her.

Her body was motionless and facedown in the grass. I knelt beside her. "Are you hurt?"

Phil flipped over.

"Here, rabbit. Here, little rabbit." She again laughed so hard that her shoulders shook.

Phil sat up and ran her fingers through her tangle of curls to comb out the dried grass.

"That was one big swampy, sure," she said.

"And you're one wild . . ." The right word to finish the sentence didn't come to me.

"One wild what?"

Phil wasn't about to let me off the hook.

"One wild . . . *chasieer of rabbeets*." My attempt at a French accent sounded ridiculous and should have embarrassed me, but it only made us both laugh.

We sat together in a circle of flattened grass and then leaned back on the ground and looked up at the late afternoon sky that was beginning to show streaks of red. I had a lot of feelings I wanted to express to Phil but holding hands seemed a better way to communicate.

★ ★ ★

The abandoned building where my car was parked had once been a mill that processed sugar and sorghum cane, Phil explained, but had not been used for decades. The family who owned it had gotten lucky in the oil business and the mill and acres of land around it were forgotten. She and her high school friends would camp out all night at the old mill and see how many fires they could count.

"Fires?"

"They have to burn the gas off the wellheads when they're pumping oil," she said. "Some nights we would count twenty or more wellhead fires. If we got brave enough, we'd go ride a pumpjack."

"A what?"

"You've seen those oil well pumps that look like a horse bending up and down to drink water?"

I nodded.

"We'd climb on and ride 'em like horses until that day we saw one of our friends almost get his leg ripped off."

Running down swamp rabbits. Riding oil-well pumps. My toughest baseball games seemed tame and ordinary.

"Take off your shirt and I'll wipe the grass off you," Phil said.

"Right here?"

"I don't bite. That Louisiana salt grass we were rolling round in can sting. You'll think you laid down in a bed of fire ants if I don't wipe you off."

Phil turned me around several times, brushing me with my cotton polo shirt turned inside out.

"I'm going to step in the mill and take off my shirt," Phil said. "You best brush that grass out from your waistband if you don't want to sit in a tub of Momma's calamine lotion all night."

Phil tugged at the tail of her plaid shirt inside her shorts and stepped behind what was left of one of the mill's interior walls. I walked outside and continued to clean the grass out from the waistband of my shorts.

"*Oo, ye, yi!*" Phil cried. "I can't get this grass off me and it's stinging. You need to help me."

"What should I do?"

"This flannel won't shake out enough. Is there anything in your car to wipe me off with?"

I ran to the car. My gym bag was at the Moreau's house and a girl couldn't be brushed off with an Esso road map. I opened the trunk and removed the urn from Mr. Spiro's duffel bag. Years of wear and many washings had left the canvas bag soft and pliable.

"Hurry," Phil said. "It's stinging some kind of bad."

I raced to the wall and offered her the cloth bag through a missing plank.

"No, no, Vic," she said, coming around the wall. "You start wiping my back and I mean every inch."

Red welts had popped up on her skin. I wiped her back with gentle strokes. Every inch, as ordered. Only one of the three hooks on her bra was fastened. Should I mention this to her? No. I was already in way over my head.

When she pulled down the waistband of her shorts in back for me to brush out the grass, I saw what I first took to be a birthmark but then recognized it as a small tattoo. A gold fleur-de-lis. The same symbol was stamped on the spines of some of Mr. Spiro's books. The French symbol with its three leaves, he once explained to me, stood for perfection, light, and life. I had never seen a tattoo on a girl, but nothing could have been more natural on the tanned back I gently brushed.

"You got any spit in you?" Phil asked.

"What do you mean?"

"I mean fill your hands with spit and rub it on my back. The sting's not easing up much."

When I ran out of saliva, Phil contributed hers into my hands. She spit like a catcher, aggressively and with volume.

"Dogs heal themselves with their spit," she said. "What's good enough for them is good enough for me."

The final cleanup duty sent us to the nearby bayou so Phil could wash the grass nettles from her shirt. I rubbed her arms and back again with the duffel bag I dipped in the bayou. We would need to be back home in no more than an hour to help her mother, she said, which should give her shirt time to dry on a tree. I shook out Mr. Spiro's duffel bag and hung it on a nearby branch.

"I do tend to get carried away and overdo it sometimes," Phil said. "I should know better than to wallow round in ripe salt grass. I reckon I'm just a *plus* girl."

"What's that?"

"*Plus* is French for 'more.' I'm always wanting a little more than is good for me."

We sat next to each other on the log, taking in the surroundings.

"I didn't kn----ow rabbits could swim," I said. "I've seen everything, now."

"You ever seen a girl in her bra before?"

"N----ot really."

"You got sisters?"

"O----nly child."

"Don't those Memphis girls wear bikinis? What's the difference?"

"T----exture, maybe." My answer sounded as ridiculous as my phony French accent. I needed to learn that some questions aren't meant to be answered.

Phil laughed. "You're one of a kind, Vic from Memphis. I don't think I should call you 'Sporty Boy' anymore."

Her eyes began another lockdown. She moved closer to me on the log.

"You might be forgetting something, but I'm not," she said. "I didn't catch a swampy, but at least I got hold of one, so I win the prize."

"What's the p----rize?"

She smiled and put her arms around my neck.

"You owe me a kiss. And I'm not talking about a sissy little Tennessee kiss. I'm talking about a bona fide Louisiana kiss."

My eleventh-grade biology teacher taught us that when a

person's body does something without thinking about it, it's called a "reflexive voluntary response." My hands gripped the warm skin of Phil's lower back near the fleur-de-lis.

In addition to never having seen a girl in a bra, I had never kissed a girl on the mouth. I had thought about it, but never had the confidence that my lips could manage an honest-to-goodness kiss given the fact that they couldn't be counted on to make the simplest of sounds.

I would need to find confirmation later, as there wasn't anything to compare it with, but my thinking was that my kiss contained a certain amount of fluency. I was confident it was of appropriate duration to make it a bona fide Louisiana kiss.

★ ★ ★

A late afternoon breeze coming off the bayou made waves in the tall grass as we drove out of the field.

"Pull through the gate and I'll chain it back," Phil said.

"Why do you have to lock the g----ate when there's not even a fence?"

"In Sout' Louisiana, you leave a gate exactly how you found it."

The certainty of her answer made my question sound foolish.

Our drive back to the Moreau house began in relaxed silence. Phil closed her eyes and leaned back to catch the late afternoon sun. I was content to sneak looks at my prettiest passenger ever. Superlative again. Pretty. Prettier. Prettiest.

Wind noise made conversation difficult with the top down, but since speaking in a louder voice helped my stuttering, I was glad when Phil opened her eyes and announced: "We need to have a talk about something." Not only was she superlative pretty, she could get right to that bush that everybody else liked to beat around.

"It's about Jimmy LaBue. I don't want you caught up in something that hasn't got a thing to do with you."

It wasn't the conversation I was expecting, but if Phil wanted to talk about Jimmy LaBue, that was fine with me.

She began with facts. Jimmy LaBue was four years older, but she didn't realize it when they had first started seeing each other. They met when he towed her boat in after her outboard wouldn't start when she was out on the river net-casting for bait. Jimmy said he would like to see her again. She put him off for six months, which took her past high school graduation. She said he was fun to be around at first, going out on the river and then on a couple of day trips to New Orleans during Mardi Gras.

"I had never met anybody who could keep up with me on the river," she said, "or who didn't seem to mind my sassy mouth and some of my funny ways."

Phil told her story like newspaper people told stories. No extra words. No fluff.

"Then he started changing," Phil said. "He started smoking stuff round me and started trying to get in my pants."

She touched my hand on the steering wheel.

"Can you pull off the road for a minute? I feel like I'm shouting this for all Louisiana to hear."

I spotted a pull-off ahead. Phil shifted in the bucket seat to face me, knees still held to her chest because of the typewriter.

"I want you to listen to me good now. About those things I just mentioned, I don't want you to get any wrong ideas. I know the way I act and my smart mouth can give people the wrong impression." She spoke firmly and directly. "But you can believe it when I tell you that I don't do those things. Not with Jimmy LaBue. Not with anybody. I may act a little wild but I'm not, what you call, easy."

She waited for me to respond.

"I understand." My reply was weak, so I added to it. "I kn----ow we just met, but I know everything I need to know about who you are."

The extra words helped. At least, they helped me. I wanted her to understand how much I meant them.

Without having to talk over the noise of the wind, Phil settled more easily into her story.

"After a while I realized things weren't right and I needed to get away from him, and that's when he started trying to give me stuff . . . and I'm not talking boxes of candy."

She paused. Her free spirit had turned into more of a hesitant spirit.

"Here's what I'm talking about. . . . One day out of the blue he gives me this new saltwater reel, still in the box. Had to cost three hundred dollars. No matter what I said, he refused to take it back. You know what I had to do?"

The wandering look in Phil's eyes let me know the story was hard for her to tell.

"I snuck it on the *Rooster* behind Daddy's back. Me oh my, I wanted to cut my ears off when I heard Daddy calling up everybody under the sun to ask if they were missing a Penn reel."

"Is there more?"

She raised her voice. "Are you kidding me? I'm just starting." For the first time, a hint of fear coated her words.

"I got in my truck one night after work and I found this box on the seat. Inside was a pair of red alligator cowboy boots that matched the ones he's so proud of."

"I g----uess they cost a lot," I said, trying to hold up my end of the conversation.

"Good waste of a gator, if you ask me. I drove straight to Saint Anthony's Church and threw them in the clothes pantry. Somebody's walking around the parish in a pair of custom-made boots from Texas that probably cost more than the car they own."

Phil lowered her head and shook it side to side.

"Then a few months ago I made the mistake of bitching to somebody at the marina about having to ride the scooter to work when our old truck broke down. Jimmy comes in next day to Maison's and orders a beer. After he leaves, I find a note and a set of car keys on the table. The note said: 'It's outside and all yours.'"

"A car?" Her story made me feel like I was following a television detective show with surprise twists and turns.

"Yes—a car. His Impala Super Sport that was only a few months old. I think that was about the time he bought that fancy truck he was following us in today."

"Where's the car now?"

"No idea. I left it where it sat, walked straight to the post office at the marina, and mailed the keys back to him."

I had more questions racing through my head, but I remembered that Mr. Spiro usually put limits on his questions beforehand to let me know he had thought carefully about what to ask.

"I have tw----o questions for you. Number one. Where does Jimmy work?" The question had a solid feel.

"You got me. When I first went out with him he said he had a good sales territory in New Orleans, but he never told me what he sold."

She looked away from me and continued. "He tries to make people think now that he's a big fisherman of some kind, but can't nobody fish out of that hot-rod boat of his with the twin V-8s and exhaust pipes sticking up in the air. That ain't no fishing boat, sure . . . and I never once smelled fish on him. It takes more than wearing a fish-guttin' knife on your belt to make you a fisherman."

I saw for the first time that my passenger, the girl who ran down swamp rabbits and teased old men with her smile, was vulnerable. My next question needed to be on the mark.

"Have you thought about talking with your parents about all this?"

"I've thought about it and maybe I'll have to, but that'll be tough for a hard-headed Cajun like me."

Phil turned toward me again.

"Can you see I told you all this because I don't want anything to happen before it's time for you to leave out of here. You probably didn't see how Jimmy looked at you today. That kind of look needs to be stayed away from. Far away."

I had seen the look and it had made an impression on me, but I wasn't about to admit it.

"Cajun men can get a little crazy when—"

I held up my hand for her to stop talking. I wanted to change the subject.

"What was that French word he c----alled me at the marina?"

"It's not important, seeing as who it came from."

"It's important to me. I'll keep on asking until you tell me."

"It's not French, I don't think, so much as it's Cajun." Phil closed her eyes and put her head on her knees. *"Bégayer* boy means 'stuttering boy.'"

My brain couldn't translate what I wanted to say. By its context, I already knew the meaning of the word, but I wanted Phil to say it, to tell me the truth to my face. To show she had confidence in me and didn't feel she had to protect me and my feelings. She looked to the horizon, shielding her eyes.

"September sun goes down fast. Momma's gonna jerk a knot in my tail if we don't get on back."

Before I thought about what I was doing, I put my hand on her untamed curls, still full of salt-grass seeds. She seemed to relax slightly.

"I'll have us home as quick as you c----an say 'swamp rabbit.' I can't wait to get to that *fais do-do.* Whatever in the world a *fais do-do* might be."

I had never learned how to console another person with that special way of saying words just the right way, but the words I needed to say to Phil and how to say them came to me clearly for a change. A hint of a smile was all I wanted from my superlative passenger. She obliged.

★ ★ ★

We drove the twists and turns along the back roads to the Moreau house without any more conversation. The wind whistling over the windshield in the little car kept us company.

In addition to being able to read maps and charts well, I had the ability to retrace my path exactly like I had come no matter how many turns or how complicated. After I got my driver's license, I found that once I had gone somewhere, I always knew exactly how to get back.

I asked Mr. Spiro once if that ability was good for anything. As usual, he answered me with a riddle disguised as a question.

"Is knowing where you have been tantamount to knowing where you are going? Dwell on it, Messenger. The exercise is well worth the investment."

I thought about sharing Mr. Spiro's riddle with Phil, but she was going through tough questions of her own. My money was on Phil that she would come up with the correct answers whatever the questions might be.

Phil was special to me and for some unknown reason, I had the feeling she was interested in me and certainly not because I was any good at chasing swamp rabbits. My luck was changing. If tossing that penny into the ceiling at the newspaper had anything to do with it, I would be happy to chuck pennies for the rest of my life.

Chapter 17

Cars and trucks three deep ringed the Moreau house. A crowd spilled out from underneath the structure along with aromas reminding me I had not eaten anything since Adrienne's leftover beignets on the drive down to Venice that morning.

Phil jumped out of the car as soon as it stopped, and, right on cue, was off and running, shouting back at me.

"Gonna change clothes. Go tell Momma I'll be right down to help her."

The concrete pad underneath the house had been transformed from a hodgepodge of odds-and-ends storage into party central. Strings of bare light bulbs hung from post to post, shining down on a half-dozen picnic tables covered with red-and-white checkered tablecloths made of plastic. Folding tables on the outside of the pad held large stainless steel pots with their contents simmering on propane stoves. Stacks of plastic bowls and plates dotted the tables along with boxes of crackers, hot sauce, and paper towels. Music played in the background on an old radio hanging from a foundation post.

She-Gene stirred one of the large pots.

"Phil said to tell you she'd be d----own to help."

"I'll believe it when I see it," She-Gene said. "That girl's only on time when there's a boat involved."

I wandered around the outside of the party. Men and women greeted me with a "how do" or a nod like they knew who I was and thought I belonged there. Kids tossed balls in the fading light and chased dogs that looked to be more interested in what was cooking than playing fetch. Captain Moreau's three charter customers sat at a table, each one taking turns spreading his hands to reveal the size of a fish caught that day. The more one of them talked, the wider he spread his hands. The men's Hawaiian shirts, gold bracelets, and sunburns were as out of place among the locals as my leather penny loafers.

I didn't know how many people lived in Venice, but it seemed a good portion of the town had turned out for Captain Moreau's birthday party and the *fais do-do*.

I saw Phil come down the front steps with a bowl heaped high with coleslaw. She had changed her shirt and shorts, the latter maybe a little longer but certainly remaining in the superlative category. Her hair was wet, making the ringlets of curls even wilder. Who came to a large party—*a fais do-do* no less—with her hair dripping wet? Philomene Moreau. It was natural. *Laissez faire.*

Phil put the bowl of slaw on top of some drink bottles being iced down in a washtub near where She-Gene stirred pots.

"What else can I do for you, Momma?" Phil hugged her

mother around the waist from behind. "You know I've just worn myself out helping you all day." I got the wink and smile. She-Gene shooed her away.

Phil made the rounds through the crowd, stopping to talk and laugh at the tables. A heavyset bearded man I had seen at the marina mussed her wet hair. She bent over him and shook it like a dog coming out of water. She circled through the crowd back to me.

"I told Momma you might want to go up and get a shower since you've been out all afternoon making me wallow in salt grass and chase rabbits."

"Wild and crazy me." I was learning that the best way to keep up with Phil was to just go along for the ride.

★ ★ ★

The muddled party noise and laughter from below came up through the floor, making the upstairs seem that much emptier. I picked up my gym bag from the living room and walked down the hall to a bathroom. I wiped off the steamy mirror above the sink. Two days of driving with the top down had left me with a deep tan on my face, but not a burn. I was glad I had one thing of my mother's. A dark complexion. If my father had been in the sun as much as I had the last two days, he would have been blistered and peeling.

I took a quick shower and shampooed my short hair with soap. My mother said that using soap to wash my hair would make it fall out prematurely. She even made me keep shampoo in my locker at the school gym, but I didn't dare take a bottle of shampoo into the shower with the guys.

I changed into a clean shirt and khaki pants from my gym

bag. No need to shave. A couple of times a week worked for me so far. I found my bottle of English Leather and splashed some on my neck and face. I was glad I had thought to bring it. I put on a little extra to make sure Phil didn't make any comments about "shrimp stink" or some such.

Gym bag in hand, I stepped out of the bathroom and noticed the door cracked at the far end of the hall. Eavesdropping was not my only bad habit. I also couldn't control my urge to see what was behind closed doors.

The room was large with two sets of bunk beds against the walls and a single bed between them. All were neatly made with the covers smoothed. Phil's rabbit-chasing clothes lay crumpled on the floor beside the single bed. A framed picture of Jesus hung on the wall and a rosary lay on top of the pillow. Underneath the picture were the words:

Blessed are they who go down to the sea in ships. — Psalm 107

Several stacks of worn paperback books stood on the floor at the side of the bed. I didn't recognize any of the titles, but their covers reminded me of the kind of westerns that my father liked to read. My snooping made me feel guilty and I hurried out of the room.

Downstairs, the lids on the pots were off and a line had formed. I thought about waiting for Phil, who was talking and laughing with the three sunburned charter customers, but my stomach overruled me when She-Gene told me to go to the head of the line. A man wielding tongs plopped an ear of corn and some boiled potatoes on my plate. A woman added a large ladle of red beans and rice. Next came something I had heard of but had never tasted. Crawfish.

Balancing two plates piled high with food, I found an empty

lawn chair in the yard near a pot with black smoke coming out of it. I shoveled in the food, which tasted even better than it smelled.

Phil came balancing a large aluminum pan containing two plates as full as mine and two overflowing bowls. She nimbly crossed her legs and sat down without spilling a drop out of the bowls. The wind shifted slightly as she took her first bite with the black smoke blowing in our direction.

"Let's move away from Daddy's skeeter buster," Phil said. "Even all that perfume you put on can't compete with Daddy's kerosene and used engine oil."

I had overdone the English Leather. I smiled at her to let her know she had caught me. Phil's rabbit-chasing expertise apparently was equaled by her sense of smell. I moved my chair away from the black smoke. Phil sat on the ground in front of me again. Her hair was almost dry and the curls restored to their natural state.

"Don't go making wisecracks about all my plates," she said. "Saves me from going back over and over. Plus, Momma said you get as much of this jambalaya as you want since you did all that peeling this morning."

Phil pulled a bottle of hot sauce from her back pocket. She ate like she did everything else—focused and fast.

She poked at my plate with her fork. "You know how to eat dem crawfish?"

Phil demonstrated with play-by-play instructions. Twist off the head. Straighten out the tail. Push it in slightly. Twist the tail and pull.

"There it be." She held the tail with a plump bite of crawfish meat on the end. She took the pink meat in her teeth and pulled it out of the tail.

"Now, don't let nobody talk you into sucking on the heads," Phil said. "Tourists think that's what you're supposed to do down here, but that's not proper Cajun, how you say, *étiquette.*"

I ate all my crawfish and started on some from her pan. As hard as you had to work for the good-tasting meat, there wasn't much of it, but I matched Phil bite for bite.

"Crawfish t----astes a little like lobster." I snagged a plump bite with my teeth. "Where do you go to c----atch a crawfish, anyway?"

"We don't really catch 'em much anymore. These probably came from the crawfish farm a little ways up in Boothville." Phil expertly twisted off a tail. "Time was when all we did was go dig 'em out of a ditch at the side of the road. We called them 'mudbugs.' I guess no one has the time for that anymore."

We twisted, pulled, and sucked in the delicious meat.

"So, how much lobster do you eat up there in Memphis?" Phil eyed me as she dipped a piece of crawfish into her jambalaya.

"Not much."

"Is your family rich?"

If that question had come from anyone else, it would have sounded out of place and rude. Coming from Phil in her matter-of-fact way, not so much.

"Not to my way of thinking. We've never had a p----arty this big at my house or with this much food . . . and we sure d----on't have anything as nice as the *Rooster Tale.*" I didn't mention my father's airplane.

I had the notion Phil wanted to ask me more questions. "What m----ade you ask that?"

"Just trying to figure you out, Vic from Memphis."

We downed our bowls of jambalaya. My eyes watered

and my nose ran from the hot sauce, which was as severe as the General's concoction for oysters, but everything tasted so good that I convinced myself I could handle the burning in my mouth.

"Is this your first time away from home on your own?"

"Is it that obvious?" I stacked my bowls and plates on Phil's aluminum tray.

"You've managed to outdo me," she said. "I've been to New Orleans, Baton Rouge, and a few places on the Mississippi coast, but that's all the traveling I've done."

"How about family v----acations?"

"Every time I go out on the *Rooster*, it's a vacation."

Phil wiped her mouth with a bandana from her back pocket.

"You don't have anything to drink," she said. "I must have burned you up with that hot sauce. You want a Dixie?"

"I've n----ever had one."

"You've never had a Dixie?"

"N----ever had a beer."

Instead of the tease I expected, Phil offered an expression of genuine astonishment.

"D----rinking age is twenty-one in Tennessee," I said in my defense.

"It's eighteen in Louisiana. We figure down here if you're old enough to get your head blown off in Vietnam, you're old enough to have a cold Dixie. Hold on. I'll be right back."

Phil rushed back and handed me the wet bottle and clinked it with hers.

"Go easy on that now. We don't want you chug-a-lugging that Dixie and gettin' all wild on us."

One of Phil's sisters came over to where we were sitting.

140

Over her pair of shorts, she wore a handmade skirt she had woven from her cattails and shrimp net.

"Momma say for you to get a block of ice from the truck and chop it for the drink tubs."

"Let me help," I said.

"Keep your seat." Phil popped up from the ground like a catcher after a foul ball. "You're gonna need your rest 'cause we're just getting started here."

Was my family rich? Mr. Spiro would have answered that by saying anything you can touch can never make you rich. What I wanted to say to Phil was that I didn't feel rich in any way in Memphis, but I had never felt so rich in my life, sitting in the Moreaus' yard with all their friends. At home, I liked typing in my room more than going to parties, but I wanted this one, this *fais do-do*, to last all night. To hear the laughter. To listen to the poetry of the language. To be filled to overflowing with the present.

I turned from the party toward the dark river I had followed for two full days.

A sentence came to me from the book where the old man was being towed out to sea by the giant fish:

The fish moved steadily and they traveled slowly on the calm water.

Had I followed the river on my own, or was something else in control and pulling me along—*steadily* and *slowly*—like the big fish? I sensed a shiver building, but then saw Phil running back to me, and the present became perfect again.

Chapter 18

Just as the meal had started without any kind of formal announcement, so did the preparation for the next part of the *fais do-do*. Men moved tables and benches from underneath the house into the yard. Women put away dishes and saw that leftover food was covered and placed in coolers. Captain Moreau unhooked a chain holding up a stack of worn sheets of plywood that were quickly laid down on the concrete pad like a tight-fitting jigsaw puzzle.

A truck backed an enclosed trailer closer to the house. Painted on the side of the trailer was a big red hat with feathers and a name, "Madam Charmaine's Zydeco Zealots," circling the hat.

Three young men in western-looking shirts hauled out large black cases containing different pieces of a drum set. Amplifiers screeched each time a guitar was plugged in. A fiddle tuned somewhere behind the trailer.

Couples—young and old—began to pair up. They began to move their feet before there was any music. The two Moreau brothers scooted close to their sisters. Captain Moreau stood behind his wife with his hands around her waist. The casual party talk and laughter had changed to a buzz of anticipation.

A squat woman wearing a red hat like the one painted on the side of the trailer strutted through the crowd that parted for her. She held her long purple skirt up with one hand. Strings of colored beads draped her neck. She grabbed the microphone with one hand and shook her tambourine above her head with the other. The tambourine silenced the crowd like a raised starter's pistol at a track meet.

"Mesdames et Messieurs. Laissez vieux Betsy souffler. Ce soir, s'il vous plaît, laissez les bons temps rouler."

Madam Charmaine spoke the strange words that somehow seemed appropriate, even though I had no idea what she had said.

I leaned toward Phil to ask for a translation, but, as usual, she was ahead of me. She whispered, "Ladies and Gentlemen. Let old Betsy blow. Tonight, if you please, let the good times roll."

The music started and dancers filled the impromptu plywood dance floor. The space underneath the house was so crowded that the dancing would have to be accomplished in shifts.

"Are you going to dance the two-step with me?" Phil lifted her feet in the air to show me a well-worn pair of black flats. "I went all out and put on shoes just for you."

"I'll need to watch for a while. I don't d----ance much, especially real dancing like everyone is d----oing here."

"You study up then. I'll be back for you." She headed for the music at a trot.

Dancing at high school parties meant standing three feet away from my date and trying to come up with gyrations that might not appear too silly. The occasional slow dance was more of a standing around while trying to figure out what to do with my hands and pretending not to be miserable.

The dancing at the Moreau house, at the *fais do-do*, was real dancing. Each couple appeared to know what was expected of them, and they did it with élan, aplomb, and éclat, as the copydesk chief would say. The movement was circular and continuous. With the way everyone glided, even in their tennis shoes and work boots, the rough plywood sheets could just as well have been a floor of polished marble. Old danced with young. The graceful danced with those who thought they were graceful. Somehow it all worked like a finely tuned fast break on a basketball court. More than couples were dancing. Neighbors danced. Families danced. An entire community danced.

Not to my surprise, Phil was in the middle of it. She took on all comers, including her younger brothers and her father, who appeared to be the partner she enjoyed the most. She waved for me to join them, but I stuck to my seat on the tailgate of a pickup. Learning the proper way to eat crawfish or to catch a swamp rabbit was one thing. Dancing the Cajun two-step was another. It appeared to be a special skill handed down through the generations only in South Louisiana.

Before the band took its first break, She-Gene led the crowd in singing "Happy Birthday" to Captain Moreau.

Phil sat down next to me on the tailgate. "I think you like that bottle of Dixie Beer more than me," she said.

The bottle was three-quarters full and warm. I had considered emptying it on the ground but was concerned the act might be taken as sacrilege in Louisiana.

"I made sure that Daddy knows to get with you about your river questions before you go to bed tonight," Phil said.

"I've been meaning to ask about that. I haven't made a----rrangements yet for a place to spend the night."

"What's a matter with you, Sporty Boy? You're sleeping here tonight." Phil slapped my hand resting on the tailgate. "Me oh my. You done gone and made me call you 'Sporty Boy' again."

"Where will I sleep?"

"In the front room . . . or you can sleep with me . . . AND . . . all my brothers and sisters." Phil whooped with laughter at her well-timed mid-sentence pause and, no doubt, the expression on my face.

For the second set, the fiddle retuned to the notes of a small accordion breathing in and out. The heavyset man from the marina with the white beard came over to where we were sitting.

"I been trying to steal me a dance with you all night, Miss Phil," the man said. "You better oblige me or I'll stop sharing my catfish bait with you."

Phil jumped off the tailgate. She put her arm around the man's thick neck.

"This is Buster," Phil said. "Only he knows the way to a girl's heart . . . hot dogs soaked in rotten chicken livers. Best catfish bait in Louisiana."

Buster stuck out his thick hand.

"I'll have her back to you soon, son," he said. "I can't keep up with her for very long anyway."

The two headed for the dance floor arm in arm.

Madame Charmaine and the accordion player kicked off a song before the drummer had a chance to take his seat for the set.

Diggy Diggy Li and Diggy Diggy Lo,
They fell in love at the fais do-do.
The rest is his-to-ry you know,
For Diggy Diggy Li and Diggy Diggy Lo.

★ ★ ★

The birthday celebration shut down as routinely as it had begun. Phil said a *fais do-do* usually went into the early hours of the morning, even on a weeknight, but folks wanted to get home to watch the television weather from New Orleans to see about the storm. She said her father had checked the weather with He-Gene in Pilottown before the party. The storm was still in the Atlantic and stalled about 350 miles east of Jacksonville, Florida.

Captain Moreau lined up dirty cooking pots on a table in the yard, turned a water hose on them and scrubbed the insides with a long-handled brush. He assigned me the job of hauling the full garbage cans to the bed of the pickup truck at the front of the house.

The crowd had been large and boisterous, but not a single piece of trash littered the yard or the pad under the house. Everyone knew to put their empty Dixie Beer bottles back in the wooden cases. When a half dozen of my friends came over to my house to swim, they left a trail of garbage behind them. In South Louisiana, you left a gate the way you found it and apparently you picked up after yourself when you were a guest at somebody's house.

As I lifted a can into the truck bed, I spotted a red truck a few hundred yards away sitting with its engine running and lights off at the side of Jump Basin Road. When I walked toward it, the truck jerked away with its tires spitting gravel. There were a lot of red trucks in Venice, and I didn't know if this was the one that belonged to Jimmy LaBue.

I had helped Phil carry loaded trays up the front steps but had not seen her since everyone had left. I ran up the stairs and into the house where She-Gene was busy at the kitchen sink.

"H----ave you seen Phil?"

"She's putting the kids to bed."

"A----re you sure?"

"Go on back and check if you want."

I rushed down the hall and opened the door without knocking. The youngest brother and sister were curled up beside Phil in her bed with their eyes closed. She was reading to them out of a worn paperback. The older two siblings flipped through comic books under small lamps in their bunk beds. Phil put a finger to her lips.

"Get outta here," she whispered. "I'll be out in a minute."

I backed out of the door.

★ ★ ★

The Captain and I stacked sheets of plywood against a wall under the house. He put the chain back around them and said he needed to go up and check the weather again.

Phil came down the stairs. "Why did you bust in my room like that?"

"I thought I saw Jimmy LaBue's truck out on the road . . . and I d----idn't know where you were."

"Even that Jimmy LaBue ain't crazy enough to mess with us at Henri Moreau's house."

"I kn----ow. I just got worried when I lost track of you."

Phil checked the front steps and pulled me over between the outboard engines attached to saw horses. We kissed. Maybe not a bona fide Louisiana kiss, but a nice one all the same.

Phil rubbed her nose on my neck. "I'm here to tell you, I do like to smell your fancy lilac water better than Daddy's skeeter buster."

"Sorry I overdid it. I never kn----ow how much of that stuff to put on."

"Talking about overdoing it, I maybe made too much out of Jimmy LaBue this afternoon," Phil said. "It just worried me the way he was acting round you, and I didn't like that look in his eyes."

I thought about saying that Jimmy LaBue didn't frighten me, but there wasn't much chance of me pulling that one off with any credibility. I had seen the eyes only once, and it was fine with me if I never had to see them again.

★ ★ ★

Like his daughter, Captain Moreau didn't have the capacity to waste words. The three of us sat on the upstairs porch in aluminum lawn chairs in the starry Louisiana night. The reflections of the few lights on shore twinkled on the surface of the moving river.

"I see a couple of issues," the Captain said. "First, there's no way I can take you out tomorrow. Those three you saw on the

Rooster today told me tonight they want to go out again in the morning even though I told them about the weather stirring. They're good customers and I can't turn down their business."

I nodded my understanding.

"Second, we need to be clear about what exactly it is you're trying to find." The Captain waved his hand at the river. "If you ask ten river pilots where they think the Mouth of the Mississippi empties out, you'll get ten different answers."

Much like the General, he explained the many complexities of the river as it flowed from New Orleans through the ever-changing passes of the bird-foot delta into the gulf. I listened closely. He must have read the disappointment on my face.

"There is one thing I can tell you," Captain Moreau said. "If my Maker appeared and told me to meet Him at the river's mouth, I know exactly where I would go. I'd be glad to take you the day after tomorrow, but that's the best I can do. It still depends on the weather, of course."

At last, I had an answer and a commitment about a specific spot from a river veteran I trusted, but I couldn't wait an extra day. I was afraid if I didn't get back when I said I would, my parents would be sending out a search party for me. Plus, I had to get back for my job at the newspaper. If I couldn't make it back on time, the job might go to someone else who didn't want it as badly as I did. I was having trouble making anyone understand the urgency of what I was trying to accomplish.

Phil read my face. She put her hand on her father's arm.

"If you tell me the spot you're talking about, Daddy, I can take Vic in the morning in the outboard."

The Captain shook his head. "Too light a craft to get you there, but let me think some and we can talk again in the morning."

The Captain stood. "I'm going in to check with He-Gene again before I turn in. If Betsy happens to change course on us, nobody will be going anywhere on the river tomorrow."

A fresh breeze had chased away the afternoon's humidity. Phil and I listened to the river with its low and continuous moan.

She patted my arm. "Daddy will come up with something. He always manages to find a way."

"I know I'm being a big p----ain to everybody down here, but I can't give up now. I feel like I'm getting close to my d----estination, to where I need to be."

Phil did her pop-up move from her chair.

"Right now, I know exactly where you need to be." She pulled me up by the arm. "You need to be downstairs giving me that dance you promised."

Stating the obvious to Phil was of no use. It didn't matter that the band was long gone. That the dance floor was full of tables now. That her proposed dance partner from Memphis didn't know how to dance.

Phil led and I followed. We held each other as we moved on the concrete floor among the tables, sawhorses, and propane tanks. The aroma of good food had been replaced by the familiar scent of Ivory soap in Phil's hair. We seemed to be dancing, but the steps didn't matter. Like Phil said, she had taken me to the place I needed to be.

★ ★ ★

The only light on when we went upstairs was over the kitchen sink. The main couch in the room was made up for me with sheets and a pillow.

"I forgot to bring p----ajamas," I said in a low voice to Phil. "I don't usually sleep in them at home."

She whispered back, "Nobody in this house sleeps in pajamas."

I didn't know how to respond, but Phil wasn't finished with me yet.

"Bonne nuit, fais de beau reves."

"What does that mean?"

Phil put her finger to my lips.

"Good night and sweet dreams."

She switched off the light and headed down the hall in the dark.

The fullness of the long day left me as tired as I felt after I had played a doubleheader, but going to sleep was not going to be easy, knowing I was so close to the Mouth of the Mississippi River. Knowing Phil was only a few steps down the hall also had something to do with it.

Chapter 19

"*Rooster* base to He-Gene. Come in."

Shortwave dreams?

"He-Gene to *Rooster* base. Over."

My sleep was deep and my head fuzzy. I had to blink my eyes a few times to remember where I was. Captain Moreau leaned in close to the radio speaker. He cupped the mic in his hand and talked softly.

"How's Betsy tracking? Over."

"On the move again and turning southwest toward the Keys, but she's a little weaker. Over."

"Think I'm okay on a half-day charter? Over."

"Coast Guard is on full monitor. Lock VHF to channel sixteen. Over."

"Check. *Rooster* out."

Captain Moreau slipped the mic back on its hook. He looked over at me on the couch. "Sorry to wake you, son, but I've learned you can't trust a hurricane named Betsy."

I pulled on my khaki pants under the cover of the sheet. She-Gene snapped on the ceiling light in the kitchen and filled a kettle with water, placing it on the stove along with a black skillet as large as a tire on my car.

"Hard to get much rest round this bunch," she said. "We'll have some coffee soon. You drink coffee, don't you?"

"Yes, ma'am. I'm learning to."

Phil bounced into the kitchen wearing what looked to be one of her father's old long-sleeved shirts. My eyes were clogged with the crud of a sound sleep, but Phil and her curls looked fresh and ready to dance all day again.

"He's been learning a bunch of new things on his trip, Momma. Told me last night the General even took him to see the hoochie-coochie shows on Bourbon Street."

"NO . . . we didn't go in," I blurted out, making me sound all the more guilty. "I t----old you they just opened the doors when we walked by." I gave Phil a stern look that did no good. She laughed.

"Don't pay that girl any mind," She-Gene said. "Phil tries to embarrass a body anytime she can."

Phil turned the flame up under the skillet.

"I'll have us some sausage sandwiches soon," she said. "And then Vic can tell us all about the hoochie-coochie girls at breakfast."

Captain Moreau rescued me.

"We'll take our coffee and sandwiches on the porch," he said, putting a captain's order in his voice. "I may have something worked out for you, Vic, if Betsy cooperates."

We ate our sausage sandwiches, which were the size of hamburgers. The Captain told us that He-Gene wouldn't be using his boat since he had to stay close to the radio all day to monitor the weather. Phil and I could take the Moreaus' old outboard downriver the nine miles to Pilottown and then switch to He-Gene's larger and more powerful boat.

"That's a good plan, Daddy," Phil said. "He-Gene's boat can handle any spot on that river, sure. I knew you'd work out something for us."

She grabbed my hand and raised it like I had won a boxing match. "Our man from Memphis is going to find that Mouth of the Mississippi River, once and for all."

Phil's excitement matched mine, but I had something else going for me. Not only was my destination close at hand, I had been promoted from "Sporty Boy" to "man from Memphis."

Captain Moreau's orders brought Phil and me back down to earth.

"Phil, I want you to go with me to dump the garbage and then on to the *Rooster* so I can show you some charts. Go get us a Thermos of coffee while I pull the truck round. She'll be back in an hour, son."

"I'd be g----lad to help with the garbage cans, and I'm pretty good at reading charts and maps," I told the Captain. His quick glance in my direction let me know that my offer was a mistake.

"She'll be back in an hour," he repeated. He tugged at his cap and went down the stairs.

I glanced at Phil for some kind of explanation of why my suggestion to join them fell so flat with the Captain. She shrugged and went to the kitchen for the coffee.

★ ★ ★

Talking with She-Gene was almost as easy as talking with her daughter, plus the fact that embarrassing hoochie-coochie comments weren't likely to show up later. The more I was around Genevieve Moreau, the more she reminded me of Phil and Adrienne. The three always seemed to move with a purpose.

After she fed her four youngest and sent them to their room to get dressed for school registration, we washed the breakfast dishes together. She-Gene asked what I would be doing when I got back home and I told her about my job at the newspaper and starting college.

"Are you having to work to pay your way through?"

"Not really, but working at the n----ewspaper is good for me seeing as how I spend too much time alone in my room." When I was comfortable with someone, words came out of my mouth that I hadn't planned on saying.

"Phil's daddy is upset that she isn't interested in college. The girl had good grades in high school without ever trying too hard." It seemed no one in the Moreau family wasted words or had anything to do with talk that was small. "He's afraid she's going to get stuck her whole life in this little fish town."

"Seems to me like a nice p----lace to get stuck." I wasn't making an excuse for Phil. I meant it.

"Maybe from the outside." She swirled the water in the sink with her hands to find more dishes. "Rich folks come down here to fish, eat fresh seafood, throw around their money, and then they go back where they come from. Only thing new that's going on down here is the oil drilling, and Henri says that will be the ruination of us all in the end."

Her voice had changed to a more serious tone. She handed me the last plate to dry.

"We stay here and try to scratch out a living and worry about getting swept away by hurricanes. Henri has a good charter business, but we couldn't make it without his pilot's pension."

"But last night everybody was having such a g----ood time."

"We have our moments, but the old ways, the family ways, are dying."

She wiped the kitchen sink with a rag. "Like that store-bought sausage we just had. Time was when all our family ate was *boudain*, that good Cajun sausage and ground rice. But nobody takes the time to make it anymore. Including me."

She dried her hands on her apron. "Soon, everybody in South Louisiana will sound, eat, and act like everybody else in the whole of the country. Might not even be such a bad thing."

"Phil likes it here," I said. "I can t----ell that she likes who she is and where she comes from."

"It's not to like or dislike. It's just who we are. But Henri thinks the time has come that the younger ones need to move on out of here. We're never going to live the lives that the ones had who came before us. The old ways won't survive."

She put her hands on the sink and looked out to the river.

"The gulf is eating away at the delta that once was our protection. It may be time to *pas la patate*."

She-Gene turned toward me quickly. "Sorry with my Cajun talk. That just means it may be time to let go of the potato."

The two sisters came down the hall arguing over which one would wear a certain blouse.

"I best get back there and keep the peace," She-Gene said. "Help yourself to more coffee or anything else you can find."

"The Captain d----idn't want me to go with him and Phil to look at his river charts," I said. "D----o you think there's some reason he might not like me?"

"He's been wanting to talk to Phil alone, but she's a hard one to set anchor on, as you probably can tell. I'd say that's all it is. He told me last night he liked the way you were bent on keeping that promise you made to your friend. Keeping your word rates high with Henri Moreau."

She hung her apron on the side of a cabinet and turned to me.

"Now don't you pay any mind to all my poor-mouthing. There never was a Moreau went to bed hungry and without a good roof overhead. We count all dem blessings, sure."

Mr. Spiro told me once that a lot of growing up had to do with "seeing with ancient eyes." My eyes looked at the Moreau house and saw only a close family, good food, dancing, and fun. If I asked my friends in Memphis what they saw when they looked at my life, they probably would say a nice house, a new sports car, and the springiest diving board in Memphis. They couldn't know how much my stutter wore on me. Or how much I wanted to know who my real father was.

★ ★ ★

Reading a book about the sea when I could smell and feel it all around me was better than reading about it surrounded by the four walls of my bedroom. I reread the part of the book I liked where the old man dreamed about the lions on the beach. I asked Mr. Spiro why the old man talked about the lions so much. My encyclopedia said there wasn't a lion of any kind in Cuba. He gave me one of his one-word answers. "Juxtaposition, Messenger." One-word answers from Mr. Spiro meant he wanted me to study that word and find out why it was important.

Juxtaposed was the way I felt when I was with Phil. Like I

really wasn't supposed to be close to her, but I was, and it all happened in such a short time and it all felt so right, juxtaposed or not.

Mr. Spiro also told me to pay attention in the book to how the old man read the sea around him. That was a lesson, he said, in how we should learn to read the world we live in and the people around us. Like knowing when to throw a change-up to a batter or learning when my father was likely to call to say he couldn't make it home to see one of my ball games.

Learning to read Phil and her emotions was exciting. I told myself I was getting better at it, and that's why I saw immediately that something was not right when she drove up to the house in the truck. She didn't jump out on a dead run. She sat and stared through the windshield. I thought about going down to meet her, but decided to let her take her own time.

The driver's door creaked open. She climbed the steps with her head down and her flip-flops in no danger of flying off.

I met her at the top of the stairs.

"Something t----ells me things didn't go well." She didn't look at me. "Any p----roblems?"

She slid past me and plopped into a chair.

"Correct. Things did not go well."

Another reading of Phil's mood told me to let her find her starting place on her own, no matter how long it took.

"Have Momma and the kids already left for school?"

"Yes. She had t----rouble starting the truck, but it finally cranked for her."

Phil nodded and scanned the river to find her words. "Daddy just laid a come-to-Jesus meeting on me."

"What d----oes that mean, exactly?"

"Meaning—exactly—I should change my ways of thinking and ask myself why I'm still living at home and wanting to work on the *Rooster*. Not surprised he wanted to talk about it, but he hurt me with his words."

The picture of Phil and her father dancing popped into my head, and how for a short time the night before I was jealous of the way they laughed and twirled each other across the plywood floor.

"You can b----e by yourself or I can listen if you want to talk about it." I didn't have a clue what she would choose.

She stood at the rail of the porch and kicked off her flip-flops. I had the feeling she was getting ready to let all of it out, like the way she opened up about her problems with Jimmy LaBue.

She started in with a flurry.

"So, to hear Daddy tell it, I'm Miss Queen Bee in my short shorts, flitting round town. 'Miss Queen Bee in short shorts'— that's exactly what he called me." A short pause. "You know what else? He says I'm mistaking what I think is popularity for folks just feeling sorry for me behind my back."

As she stood at the railing, her disbelief tumbled over more to anger.

"Oh, and this is the best one. I'm like one of those bright-colored pinwheels that people get at the parish fair and then forget about as soon as they get home."

"H----ard for me to h----ear your father saying those things to you."

"Well, hear it . . . 'cause that was his words to me."

If there was going to be any crying, this would be the time, but Phil didn't seem to know about tears. She jerked open the screen door, went inside, and came back out with a bottle of Dixie Beer.

"Have one if you want," she said. "They're in the icebox."

"D----id you say anything back to him?"

"Oh yeah, and I got bit good in the butt again. I told him I guess he didn't appreciate me staying round to help with the kids, and you know what he said then?"

I shook my head.

"He said, 'What makes you think your mother and I are not capable of raising our children without your help?'"

She dropped her head.

"I didn't think he could hurt me any more than that, but then he stuck the gaff hook in me good." The fire in her eyes was dying. "He told me the real reason I don't leave home is because I'm too afraid that I can't handle what's out there."

Phil opened the screen door.

"I need some time alone," she said. "We'll have to leave for Pilottown before too long. Everybody at the marina is getting their panties all in a twist listening to the weather radio about the storm."

"Y----ou don't have to b----other with taking me out on the river. I can find someone else at the marina," I said, but I was talking to an empty room through the screen door.

I shook the porch railing in frustration, so hard that the almost-full bottle of Dixie Beer toppled off and shattered on the crushed shells on the ground. Phil needed some comforting words from me, and I had nothing to give her. Not only could I not make small talk, I couldn't make big talk, the important words that someone needed to hear at crucial times.

Chapter 20

Phil lazily shifted through the gears of the truck. I had not ridden with her but had pegged her as someone who would drive as aggressively and as fast as she did everything else. I carefully worded my sentences to explain that I had put my extra money in the duffel bag with the urn and that I could pay someone at the marina to take me out on the river if she could tell me about the place where her father said I could find the Mouth of the Mississippi River.

Wrong approach. Wrong words.

"Oh sure. All I need now is for Henri Moreau to see his daughter run out on a rich boy from Memphis who drove all the way down here so he could keep a promise to a dead man."

The combined look of frustration and fear on Phil's face was the same kind I had when words spewed from my mouth twisted and confused, but I couldn't let her mean words go unchallenged.

Even sensing that she wanted to take back her words, I couldn't stop myself from lashing back at her.

"And d----on't forget . . . a s----puttering boy at that."

My cruel words to her tasted bad in my mouth. When I threw my hardest fastball, it went to the outside of the plate, never inside. I was always afraid of hurting someone. Words were no different. I tried to use them carefully after being stung so many times myself. Phil didn't intend for her words to come out the way they did. I knew that she was confused, but I also knew that self-pity didn't fit her well. I wanted her to leave that way of thinking and come back to me in the way that was her nature.

She stomped on the brake pedal.

"Oh, Vic, I'm just talking out of my head. You know I didn't mean that."

I pretended to look in the truck's side mirror. I couldn't make myself face her.

"Please forgive me," she said. "Truth is, the river is where I need to be. With you."

I adjusted the mirror. Phil scooted toward me. I sensed her lean in and then snap herself back under the steering wheel.

"I have no right," she whispered to herself. And then to me: "I'm so sorry for what I said."

Roller coasters never suited me. The feelings at the bottom of the ride never matched the anticipation at the top, and the plunge in the middle was always too confusing to take in. My thoughts slammed into one another the rest of the way on the short drive to the marina. Phil parked the truck near the stairs that led up to the office. When she reached to turn off the ignition, the roller coaster plunged and I heard myself say, not in a whisper: "I have a right."

I grabbed Phil's face with both hands and kissed her on the mouth.

My speech therapist once showed me in her office a diagram that explained how it took more than one hundred small muscles in the area of the tongue and the mouth to produce a single vocalization. Every one of those muscles got a good workout when I kissed Phil. Then, she took over for me and seemed to do the kissing.

At some point, air became more of a problem than muscle fatigue. When we let go of each other, Phil fluffed out the curls on the side of her head where I had grabbed her. It was the first time I had seen her fuss with her hair. She seemed to have joined me on the roller-coaster ride.

She opened her door and stepped to the curb, hesitated, and returned to the window of the truck.

"Are you trying to convince me not to call you a 'boy' anymore?"

Phil slapped the top of the cab so hard that it made me jump. She headed up the stairs two at a time. I stayed in the truck a little longer to make certain my roller coaster was going to stay on its tracks.

★ ★ ★

Hurricane Betsy was the sole topic of conversation in the marina office. Buster fiddled with ribbons of tinfoil on a set of rabbit ears on a small television. Men standing at the counter repeated to one another what the weather forecasters had just said.

The storm was erratic and massive, six hundred miles from

tip to tip with an eye that was forty miles wide. After stalling in the Atlantic, highly unusual for a hurricane on a northerly track the men said, Betsy had turned southwest. The Florida Keys braced for a major hit. Would it continue on its southwest course, as some predicted, and stall itself out in the lower gulf that had slightly cooler waters?

Phil motioned for me to join her at the chart of the Lower Mississippi River that took up one of the walls in the marina office. The excitement had returned to her voice. Maybe it was the hurricane talk, but I liked to think the kiss in the truck that I had not planned had something to do with it. Acting on the spur of the moment was not something I normally did, but I was growing to like the feeling of the spur as well as the moment.

"This is what we'll do," she said. "We'll take the little outboard to Pilottown, running just east of the main channel but close enough to catch a good current. We should get there in less than an hour."

She traced the route on the chart with her finger.

"At Pilottown we'll switch to He-Gene's boat with the twin outboards. We'll head straight to this spot." She tapped the chart. "As Daddy sees it, somewhere around here is that perfect place you're trying to find for Mr. Spiro."

Phil had packed a small ditty bag with the only things we would need, she said—a handheld compass and a pair of binoculars. She would triangulate by using two buoys, which she pointed out on the chart. I didn't understand the particular details, but didn't want to question my river guide who had found her new sense of purpose. I concentrated on the chart.

"You want to know if I'm going to take you to the right place, don't you?"

I nodded. Phil was all the way back on top of her game, reading my thoughts almost as soon as they came to me.

"I'm going to tell you all about where we're going, but I want to be on the river alone with you when I do. Not with this loud bunch of yahoos in here." She put her finger on the wall chart again. "Only my daddy and I know about this place that is so simple in its beauty."

The same daddy earlier in the morning who had . . . but I dared not go there with Phil.

★ ★ ★

Buster walked behind us to the slips where the small boats were docked. He didn't look too worse for wear after a long night of dancing and drinking beer.

"Does Captain Henri know you're headin' out this morning with that Betsy still shuffling her feet out there in the gulf?"

"Daddy's already out a lot farther than we're going." Phil untied the outboard's dock line.

"I knowed that, Miss Phil, but he's on the *Rooster* with a good radio, and you're fixin' to ship out in this little scuttle with nothin'."

"We're only going to Pilottown, Buster, and then we'll switch to He-Gene's boat that has a good radio. We'll be back soon, sure." Phil's accent ramped up when she talked to Buster.

"You knowed better than to tease dat river, Miss Phil."

Buster got no response. He shrugged his shoulders and headed back to the marina office. It was evident that he also had experience in losing arguments with this strong-willed sailor.

Phil set the choke on the engine, squeezed the bulb on the fuel line, and yanked the starter cord. The old outboard smoked

and chugged to life on the third pull. The small aluminum boat with its V-hull had two bulkhead seats. Phil sat in the rear on a flotation cushion, steering with one hand on the twist throttle. My seat was on a sun-cracked cushion in the middle of the boat. Between us were two orange life jackets covered in green mold. Mr. Spiro's duffel bag rested on them. Phil stowed the ditty bag behind her seat, in a wooden box next to the gasoline tank.

As Phil slowed the boat to adjust the carburetor, I glanced back at the marina to see Buster on the dock waving in our direction with both arms. I motioned for Phil to turn around. She waved back at him.

"I do think old Buster is sweet on me." She eased the throttle up to what I took to be full speed. Buster continued to wave to us until I could no longer see him.

The outboard engine, coupled with the downriver current, pushed the boat at a good clip. I wanted to turn to see the wind push Phil's curls back and expose her perfect face, but she had a job for me. I was to be on lookout for any river flotsam that might pop up in front of the boat too late for Phil to see. She told me to throw out either hand and she would swerve that way.

Even though I had lived in Memphis all my life, I had never been out on the Mississippi River, unless you counted escorting a Miss Cotton Carnival contestant onto a barge while I was dressed in a silly rented tuxedo. Mr. Spiro, however, talked to me about the river on the days we caught a city bus downtown to Front Street and walked over to Mud Island, our favorite spot to watch the Mississippi roll by.

Mr. Spiro saw more than simply what was going on at the surface of the river. He would point out a dead tree with a huge root ball caught in the current heading toward an innocent-looking swirl of water. The tree would disappear, sucked down by a powerful whirlpool like it was a toothpick. We watched for the tree to pop up somewhere downriver—fifty yards or five hundred yards. Only the river knew where it would let go. He told of towboats with ten-thousand-horsepower diesel engines entering a bend in the river at the wrong angle in high water, and being pulled along helplessly like a toy in a bathtub until the river released it in its own good time. "Never fight the river, Messenger. The river will always win."

"Some big trees sticking out up ahead," I shouted back to Phil. My words tumbled out without stutters. I loved to shout when there was a proper time for it.

She eased back on the throttle and came about to get a better look.

"A long bar juts out there," she said. "We're about halfway to Pilottown. I'm going to pull in to that eddy for a minute." Even not knowing much about the river, I had no doubts about Phil's ability to handle a boat.

"That small log will anchor us if I can run up on it," she said. "Hold on."

She twisted the throttle and the bow of the boat came to rest perfectly on top of the smooth log. I stood to congratulate Phil on her tricky maneuver. Big mistake. The boat rocked to one side and the other as I fought to get my balance. I dropped hard to my knees to keep from dumping both of us into the river.

"Should have told you this kind of boat can flip to one side when the bow is out," Phil said. "Are you okay?"

My khaki pants were ripped and blood trickled from a small cut on the side of my knee. Phil took her bandana from her back pocket.

"Tie this round your knee," she said. "The cut doesn't look all that deep."

Phil scanned the river with her binoculars.

"Did you see Jimmy LaBue's truck and fancy trailer when we pulled in at the marina?"

No. That was about the time my brain was going on its roller-coaster ride. I shook my head.

"He usually doesn't put in at the Venice marina. Can't imagine why he's out on the river round here, unless he's trying to give the fish a heart attack with those loud V-8s."

She lowered the binoculars.

"So, what have you heard about Pilottown, Louisiana?"

"Only that it's the t----own that He-Gene lives in."

"Well, first, a person can't live 'in' Pilottown. You kind of live 'on' it. Pilottown mostly sits on pilings above the river and wetlands. He-Gene is the only full-time resident now. Daddy said it once had a general store and even a barroom with dances on Friday nights, but the gulf is eating it away."

Pilottown had a zip code, but no post office now. He-Gene not only worked for the Crescent River Port Pilots' Association but also for the Louisiana Department of Wildlife and Fisheries, Phil said. He took care of the Pilottown generators and monitored radio traffic for the Coast Guard, the Bureau of Narcotics, and the Plaquemines Parish Sheriff's Department.

"Your uncle sounds like he keeps busy," I said.

"Everybody wonders exactly what all he does all day out there. He doesn't tell us much, even the family, but I'll say he knows what's going on. He's the sharpest man on the river . . . other than Daddy, of course."

The boat twisted in the current but the bow stayed perched out of the water, resting on its log.

"So, how far from P----ilottown is this special place your daddy talked about?"

Phil scooted down to the floor of the boat, stretching out her legs. She tucked her flotation cushion behind her for a backrest and told me to do the same with mine.

"I'm going to tell you a beautiful story about where we're going."

She dabbed at the cut on my knee with the bandana.

"When daddy brought the *Rooster Tale* home almost ten years ago, he said he wanted to take me to a special place. Even though I could barely see over the wheel, he let me pilot the new boat all the way to the Southwest Pass, then he took over and told me to go to the foredeck to get ready to drop anchor."

Lying next to Phil in the boat made it difficult for me to concentrate, so I closed my eyes and made myself hear every word as she spoke above the rush of the river.

"Daddy came to the bow and put his arm around me and told me to look at the horizon and then bring my eyes down slowly. When I did, I took the shimmer on the water to be the reflection of the low sun behind us, but then realized it was fish jumping. Beautiful little silvery fish. Mullet."

"What k----ind of fish is that?"

"It's a bait fish. Folks in Mississippi call them 'Biloxi Bacon' and tell silly mullet jokes, but I love the cute little things."

I peeked and saw Phil's eyes were closed, but she was smiling in a way I had never seen.

"Mullet are saltwater fish that aren't sure they should be fooling round with the freshwater of the river, but Daddy said it called to them in a siren's song they couldn't resist. They knew in their heads they should be sticking to the saltwater plan that the good Lord had intended for them, but they just couldn't say no in their crazy little mullet hearts."

Phil sat up.

"I watched them fly out of the water, colliding in midair and doing somersaults. Daddy called it the 'mullet dance.' He said the longer we idled in the river, the higher the mullet would jump because the vibration of the *Rooster's* engines made them curious and inspired them to explore even more. They jumped higher and higher."

She leaned back on her cushion and looked at me.

"Daddy asked me what the shape of their jumps reminded me of. I had to think a minute, but then I saw it. The tail of a rooster."

Phil drew the shape with her finger on the front of my shirt.

"As far as I know, I'm the only one who knows what Daddy meant by naming his boat the *Rooster Tale*. He saw fit to share his tale of the mullets only with me. Daddy said this one spot on Southwest Pass was the one place he had seen the mullet do their special dance."

"But why—"

Phil knew my question before I could finish it.

"Don't you see, Vic? The mouth of the river is where its freshwater meets the saltwater of the gulf. We'll know the exact location of the mouth of the river when we see the mullet dance."

Chapter 21

The intensity of her story and the flow of the river rushing through the patchwork of floating logs had put us both into a daydream. I took deep breaths of the Ivory soap in Phil's hair. It took three blasts from a sea-going freighter struggling against the current in midchannel to get us thinking about moving downriver again.

Phil yanked the starter cord.

"All hands on deck. Next port of call: Pilottown," she announced. "All ahead, full." Phil changed moods with the swiftness that a swamp rabbit changed directions.

The cut on my knee had stopped bleeding. I untied the bandana to wash out the blood and noticed the pattern on the cloth was the fleur-de-lis.

Perfection. Light. Life.

Another freighter in the main channel came into view and then a third one soon after.

"I've never seen them bunched up like that," Phil shouted above the noise of the outboard and the bow slapping the water. "They usually stay at least four or five miles apart. He-Gene must be having a time trying to get all his pilots on board."

We skirted an outcropping of marshland. Phil dodged floating debris more out of instinct than from my directions. It was difficult for me to tell what was land and what was a thick layer of muck floating on top of the water. Small islands turned out to be only patches of river grass.

We crossed the wide mouth of a pass on our left, and for the first time I thought I could see far out into the Gulf of Mexico. I turned and pointed in that direction. Phil shook her head and pointed straight ahead.

A half dozen small white buildings on pilings rose out of the river—Pilottown. The structures hung above the river on a mishmash of uneven boardwalks. Several tall radio antennae whipped in the breeze like large river cattails. Behind the smaller buildings were larger ones that appeared to be abandoned, some with their roofs gone.

We saw an outboard boat heading away from Pilottown at high speed and then turn up into the river's current. Phil, looking through her binoculars, said she recognized the operator as one of He-Gene's pilots. She waved but couldn't get his attention.

Phil eased back on the throttle as we approached the dock.

"Welcome to . . ."

I twisted on my cushion. Phil shook her head slowly.

"Something's not right." Her searching eyes revealed more than her words.

We pulled in to a slip next to the only boat bobbing up and down at the floating dock. Metal footlockers with different kinds of government insignias filled the deck of the boat. Smaller containers on top were lashed down with heavy yellow lines crisscrossing back and forth. Somebody and their belongings were on the move.

When you're on the river in a boat, there's always a wind, but now we were docked and the wind had a power of its own.

"Hey, Phil," a man shouted from an overhead crosswalk. "Thank God you're here."

"What's going on, He-Gene?" Phil shouted back.

"I radioed the marina, but they said I just missed you." The ramshackle stairs swayed as He-Gene scrambled down to dock level with a large walkie-talkie in his hand.

"I have orders to evacuate." He-Gene's khaki shirt and pants were soaked with sweat. "Betsy has turned northwest in the gulf and is tracking straight for us. You and your friend need to head back to the marina immediately. I just sent my last pilot home."

"Is that why all the freighters are stacked up?"

"Just sent the last one through. Coast Guard has closed the river."

"Have you radioed the *Rooster*?"

"As soon as I heard. Henri is on his way back in to Venice. He told me to turn you around immediately."

He-Gene and Phil discussed the situation like the river veterans they both were. Going back upriver, we should hug the west bank where the current was the weakest. He would radio both the *Rooster* and the marina before he shut off the generators and packed up the last of the radio equipment. Everybody would know we were accounted for and were headed back in.

"When are they expecting Betsy to come ashore?" Phil asked He-Gene, her question revealing more calmness than I was feeling.

"Not sure. Depends on how much the warmer waters of the gulf speed her up, but the fore-winds and storm surge will start later today."

Static on He-Gene's handheld receiver interrupted their conversation. He raised his hand and put the radio to his ear.

"The sheriff's department just ordered Venice evacuated," he said.

"Can we haul anything back for you?" Phil asked.

"Heavens no," He-Gene said. "You don't need added weight going upriver with that small outboard. I've got a few more things to do and then I'm closing it down. I'll see you at the marina . . . or at the house."

He-Gene looked at me for the first time. We had not been introduced.

"Sorry to spoil your plans, son, but we can't mess with hurricanes out here, exposed as we are." He climbed the stairs and looked back at Phil. "Henri said he would decide when he got in what he would do with the *Rooster*. He may want you to help him take it upriver, depending on how Betsy is tracking."

He-Gene scrambled back up the flimsy set of stairs and was gone. Phil and I sat in the small boat. I waited for her to crank the outboard. She surveyed the tumbling sky in all directions.

"I feel the wind changing a little to more out of the southeast, but the sky's not doing much yet," she said. "I think I have a plan for our Mr. Spiro."

"Getting back to the marina needs to be our only plan," I said over the wind in a louder voice than normal. "I'm pretty sure that Mr. Spiro would say the same thing."

Phil seemed to have a hard time listening when she was focused on what was in her head. She agreed that the trip to the end of the Southwest Pass was out of the question, but she said she had another idea. Both the Corps of Engineers and the Coast Guard designated Mile Marker 0 at Head of Passes as the official Mouth of the Mississippi River, even though it was miles from the Gulf of Mexico and from the dancing mullets. She explained that since we had to cross the main channel anyway to get over to the west bank, it wouldn't take much time to go downriver a little ways where I could lay Mr. Spiro to rest.

I shook my head. "Since we can't go to your father's special place, we should head straight back like He-Gene told us to."

Phil cranked the outboard and said, "Who's the captain of this vessel?"

She twisted the throttle and we headed out into the river.

The rhythm of the bow slamming into the water brought back to me two sentences with their own rhythm that I remembered typing from the book:

If there is a hurricane you always see the signs of it in the sky for days ahead, if you are at sea. They do not see it ashore because they do not know what to look for. . . .

★ ★ ★

The sound of the outboard changed as we moved into the current of the main channel. The small engine didn't have to strain going downriver in the swift current. Phil looped the strap of the binoculars around her neck. I grabbed the sides of the boat with my arms outstretched.

I could see already how the river branched out into the different passes the General and the Captain had told me about. Southwest Pass. South Pass. Pass a'Loutre. Looking at a flat piece of paper on a table was not anything like looking at the real thing, like typing out a story was different from life happening around you.

"Are you sure this is a good idea?" I shouted.

"We're almost there. Hang on."

The current in the main channel grew more turbulent as it prepared to split apart to find the different passages to the gulf. I sat in the middle of my seat on the cushion, leaning to one side and then the other as the boat made its way in the confused river.

Phil threw one of the orange life jackets to me. "Put this on. We're getting close. I'm going to swing round and hold us against the current when I think we're about even with the marker." She held the binoculars in one hand and steered with the other. I put my head and arms through the life vest.

Many times I had played out in my head how I would take four separate handfuls of ashes from the urn, releasing each one into the air as I said one of Mr. Spiro's four special words that made up his Quartering of the Soul. I wouldn't stutter since each word started with the nice *s* sound and, anyway, I planned to shout them as loud as I could. My plans had never included the ferocious chop of the river and a hurricane in the Gulf of Mexico.

I put the duffel bag onto my lap and removed the urn. The tape held the top securely like the manager at the funeral home promised it would. Too securely. The urn had been in the hot trunk of my car for more than a week. The tape had melted into a goo that had hardened again.

Phil brought us around and backed off the throttle, holding the bow steady against the current. She nodded. I picked at the sticky tape with my fingernails as the boat bucked.

A new sound came from the river at the place with the strange name—Head of Passes. A loud sound. A harsh sound. Loud and moving closer. I didn't look up. I concentrated on getting the top off the urn.

"No," Phil cried.

I turned on my cushion to see a sleek boat with chrome exhaust stacks emerge from an outcropping of trees, heading straight for us at high speed and throwing up a violent wake. Even against the strong current, the bow of the boat's planing hull was out of the water and charging toward us. Phil twisted open the throttle. The outboard's propeller dug down into the river, raising the bow. The boat shot ahead, throwing me off my seat and back into Phil—and the duffel bag and urn into the river. Phil let go of the throttle grip to get her balance. With the sudden deceleration, water rushed in over the stern. The outboard engine hissed and sputtered to a stop. When I stood to try to locate the urn in the river, the speedboat raced by, missing our boat by inches. The giant wake heaved our small craft into the air. And launched me into the river.

When you dive into a swimming pool, you know what's coming and it's no big deal. When you are thrown into the river, your whole body hits hard and everything is out of place. The water felt neither warm nor cool. All I could feel was the sense of being captured and a sense of loss.

Losing the penny loafer on my right foot was my first sensation under water. I felt out of balance. I kicked off my other shoe as the life vest pulled me to the surface. Phil waved her arms wildly and shouted from the boat. I couldn't understand her shouts. The current pushed us swiftly downriver through all manner of flotsam and dead trees. Upriver, the loud boat sped away, its name painted in gold script letters on the transom— *Crazy Eights*.

Phil yanked the starter cord with all her might. Again and again.

"Try to grab a snag," I heard her shout. "I'll come get you."

I twisted and turned in the river as it carried me. Phil continued pulling the starter cord without success, but I realized that Phil and the boat were staying about the same distance away from me. We were both caught evenly in the current. I looked downriver and spotted the urn, floating toward the main current of the river and out to sea. I swam for it. Swimming against the river's current would have been useless. Swimming with it gave me the sensation of flying over the water. Like a mullet.

Messenger.

I swam harder toward the sound of my name. The one that only Mr. Spiro used.

What should I do, Mr. Spiro?

I reached the urn bobbing in the current and wrapped both arms around it. *Don't fight the river, Messenger. The river will always win.*

I closed my eyes, hugged the urn, and gave myself over to the fast-moving water.

Chapter 22

My right arm hugged the urn against my chest. With my left hand, I gripped a branch of a fallen tree with a few of its roots still anchoring it to the bank.

Blood streamed down my face and into my eyes. I didn't have a free hand to wipe it away, but through the blur I could make out Phil as she steered her powerless boat into a small eddy by using her seat cushion like a rudder. She wrestled the boat between logs to the bank a few yards from where I hung on to the tree.

"Stay still," Phil said when she reached me. She wiped the blood out of my eyes with the tail of her shirt. I thought of good questions to ask. Where was the blood coming from? If I was cut, how bad was it? Or maybe just one big question—what happened?—but I couldn't form the words in my mouth, and it wasn't because of a stutter or a sputter.

After Phil dragged me through the shallow water to a spot on the bank, she answered some of the questions I could not ask.

"Your head hit the rail of the boat. You have a nasty gash we have to do something about."

Phil put her life jacket under my head for a pillow. She took off her shirt, folded it several times and put it on my head.

"Give me the urn," she said.

I had trouble straightening my arm to let go of it. The urn seemed almost attached to me. She put the urn in the boat and then grabbed my arms and raised them over my head.

"Now, it's important you keep pressure on your head with both hands," she said. "Stay completely still. I'll be right back."

I turned my head to one side and squinted to see Phil in her bra slide down into the river near the boat.

She tied the anchor line around her waist, and for a reason I could not come up with, she dove under the surface. The line tightened in the current. She finally surfaced out in the river with two handfuls of mud and made her way back to the bank.

"Phil . . ."

"Stop talking now. You're going to be okay. Just stay quiet."

Phil kneaded the dark river-bottom mud back and forth in her hands and packed it on my head. The coolness of the mud felt good. She tore both sleeves from her shirt and tied them together for a bandage to keep the mudpack in place.

"You're looking like a pirate now." She put on what was left of her blood-soaked shirt. "I better keep my clothes on 'cause I don't want you getting ideas about me out here on the river." She smiled but it wasn't her honest kind of smile.

The pulsating pain in my head increased the longer I lay on the bank. I could feel each throb as it approached in a steady rhythm.

The river was wide at Head of Passes. I looked at the

out-of-commission boat and wondered if it was about the size of the one that the old man fished from in the Gulf Stream.

"Do sharks ever come this far up in the river?" The question came out of my mouth in a way that made it seem like I was not the one who was talking.

Phil gave me an odd look.

"Just the bull sharks that can live in freshwater." She tightened the bandage on my head. "If you're needing to worry about something, might be best to worry about gators instead of sharks."

"I haven't seen an alligator since I've been down here."

"That's how they like it." Phil smiled. She changed the tone of her voice. "I'm just foolin' with you. If there's a hurricane on the way, the gators aren't going to be the least bit interested in the two of us."

Phil had used the word "hurricane" for the first time. She changed the subject.

"Jimmy had the look of a wild man when he sidewashed us. Probably high on something."

"Was he trying to hit us?"

"No. That would have messed up his pretty boat. He wanted to scare us, sure." She wiped a trickle of blood from my eye. "When Daddy hears what that *couyon* did, the *Crazy Eights* will find itself on the bottom of the river . . . with Jimmy LaBue likely in it."

"How did I get to the bank?"

"That dead cottonwood tree with the big root ball reached right out and grabbed you as you were floating by. It held you long enough for me to get to you and pull you up on the bank."

Phil explained that our outboard engine had sucked in water

from the backwash and she was going to take off the cowling so the carburetor could dry out before she tried to crank it again.

"What if it won't start?"

"Then you, me, and Miss Betsy will have us a double date tonight." She smiled but saw I wasn't smiling.

"Don't worry. Daddy and He-Gene will come for us long before Betsy gets here. No need to worry about that, sure."

When I tried to raise my head to wash the mud off my arms and legs, the river turned upside down in front of me. I felt like I was going to fall even though I was lying down. Phil eased my head back onto the muddy bank. She cupped water in her hands and washed me as best she could.

"Tell me this," she said. "Why did you swim for the urn instead of toward the bank?"

I had the answer, but how could I explain? I pressed the mudpack on my head with both hands to try to stop the throbbing.

"My I-Powers were at odds," I said finally.

The confused look on Phil's face matched my own confusion of how to explain what I had just said. I knew what I meant by "I-Powers," a lesson that Mr. Spiro had taught me about "intellect" and "intuition," but my brain felt like it was full of the mud that Phil had just pulled from the bottom of the river.

I reached out to wipe a speck of river trash from Phil's cheek, but my hand wouldn't go where my brain told it to go. I closed my eyes.

I heard *Messenger* again from far away. *Don't fight the river.*

Once more, I let myself float away.

★ ★ ★

Phil blew hard over and over again into the recesses of the small engine. I wanted to do something to help her, but my body was shaking so badly I knew it was no use. Any sudden movement of my head caused me to see double. My brain couldn't make sense of what I was seeing with my eyes. The pounding in my head had turned into giants slamming home runs.

She snapped the small engine's cowling back in place.

"Three pulls and it'll crank. *Garanti.*" Her smile and her accent made me want to believe her. She gripped the starter cord with both hands and yanked. After a dozen or so pulls, each one more aggressive than the previous, the engine coughed and then chugged to life in a feeble idle. She played with the small screws on the carburetor until the engine smoothed out.

"I'll help you into the boat if you can slide into the water," she said.

I eased down the mud of the riverbank and grabbed the boat rail.

"Water is f----reezing," I mumbled.

Phil grabbed my arms. "I'm going to lean away from you and pull. See if you can throw one leg over the side and roll in."

On the third try I rolled into the boat.

"D----d----d----oes a hurricane m----m----ake the water c----c----older?" For once I could blame my stuttering on my teeth that wouldn't stop chattering.

"Water temp is the same," Phil said in a matter-of-fact tone. "You're probably just running a little fever."

In what seemed like a realignment of different parts of my brain when I settled into the boat, I had a strange desire to talk. To say anything. To babble. Sentences ran through my head before I could capture and make any sense of them.

"Phil, I have a truth to tell you."

"Okay," she said with some hesitation. "What's this truth of yours?"

"You're twice as pretty now as I've ever seen you."

She shook her head.

"You need to sit down in front of me to cut down on wind resistance." The order sounded like one from Captain Moreau.

"Know why you're twice as pretty? I see two of you."

My attempt at a joke was lame, but there was that truth to consider. She was beautiful and I had been seeing two of her like I saw two of everything else. I had no control over what I was saying. I couldn't even tell if I was stuttering.

The engine labored as we continued into the teeth of the current in the main channel. Shivers ran through my body. I folded my arms across my chest. Phil pressed her legs against my shoulders as I sat in the bottom of the boat in front of her. She steered with one hand and with the other hand applied pressure to the mudpack on my head. I gripped the urn between my legs.

The current eased a bit when we reached the shallows running along the west bank. Phil dodged logs and snags with the throttle wide open. Clouds out of the south raced above us and the sky darkened. Phil kept her free hand firmly on my head. The throbbing kept time with the bow as it slammed into the river. I could feel the blood in my head trying to find new pathways, like the river trying to find new routes to the gulf at Head of Passes.

I wanted to tell Phil how Mr. Spiro had told me not to fight the river, but the words wouldn't line up in my head. And then I remembered the nonfiction that Mr. Spiro wasn't really here. He was only in the urn.

I felt Phil's strong hand on my head and did the only thing I could do. I closed my eyes.

Chapter 23

Phil spoke from behind what seemed like a wall, with me on the other side in a dark room. "I knew they'd be looking for us."

"Wh----at, wh----at d----o you see?" My eyes had been closed for most of the trip upriver. I blinked several times to try to get them to focus. The small engine labored.

"I see Daddy and He-Gene on the dock with their binoculars. I think I see Ray Patton, too."

"The G----eneral? Are we in New Orleans?"

"No, we're back at the marina. I've never seen the place so crowded. Boats are stacked up everywhere waiting to haul out."

"H----ave I b----een asleep?"

"More passed out than sleeping." She squeezed my shoulders with her legs. "Hold on for just a few more minutes."

Phil steered away from the shelter of the riverbank for a more direct route to the marina.

"Feel that?"

"No." I didn't shake my head for fear my mudpack would come off.

"The current has eased in the main channel. I can feel it in the throttle." She took her hand on and off the rubber grip. "Old timers round here say the start of a storm surge will slow the current, even make the river run backward. We might be in for a good blow from Betsy."

The marina was a football field away.

"Can you climb up on your seat?"

I gripped the urn to my chest. I managed to lift myself up on the seat with one hand.

Phil momentarily took her hand off the throttle and stretched both arms straight out. She waved them in large circles like she was a bird trying to take off. Captain Moreau signaled back from the dock by raising one hand above his head and making tight circles with it.

"What was that all about?"

"Just letting them know we're going to need first aid. Uncle Gene keeps a kit in his boat."

The Captain motioned for his daughter to pull in to the dock, where he hung on to a ladder with his feet in the river. Phil throttled back and cut the engine.

"What happened, Philomene?" the Captain said.

"Help me get Vic out of the boat first," she said, letting me hear for the first time the concern in her voice.

I handed the urn to the Captain and reached for the ladder, but missed it on my first try. Phil steadied the boat against the pilings. I reached out again and the Captain grabbed my arm. My bandage fell down over one eye and the mudpack, which had dried into a solid cake of blood, dropped into the river.

The General kneeled on the dock and grabbed my other arm. "You didn't get sliced up by a propeller, did you?"

"It's okay," I said. "I don't think it's b----leeding anymore."

The General pulled a white handkerchief from his back pocket, patted my head and showed a dark circle of fresh blood. He put the handkerchief back on my head and placed my hand on it.

"Keep pressure on it," he said.

Phil leaned over the side of the boat to wash off the blood that covered her arms and hands.

"Are you hurt?" I heard Captain Moreau ask his daughter.

Phil shook her head. "It's not my blood."

The General guided me to a wooden bench built into the dock railing and helped me lie down. He pulled off his top shirt, wadded it, and made a pillow for me. He-Gene came running down the dock with a large first-aid kit.

"Uncle Gene was a hospital corpsman in the Navy," Phil said. "You're in good hands now."

He-Gene pushed and probed the skin of my head that seemed to have a loose flap on it. He informed everyone that the cut ought to be sutured but had already started to close on its own.

"I'll have to irrigate this," He-Gene said. "You hold his head, Henri, and you get his arms, General."

Before I could say that none of that would be necessary, He-Gene poured a liquid into my wound. I opened my mouth to scream, but the pain took away my air like the worst vocal block of all time. The only option was to do once again what I seemed to be getting good at. I closed my eyes.

The General sat at the end of the bench with his hand on my outstretched legs.

My first thought when I came back to my senses was that someone had been cleaning typewriters with my alcohol and cotton swabs.

I turned my head toward the river. "Where's Phil?"

"Good. Glad you're back with us, Son Vic." The General patted my bare feet. "Phil and her father took the skiff over to the *Rooster*. You'll see her again soon."

The events of the day and the General's presence weren't coming together in my head yet.

"Are you supposed to be here?" I asked the General.

"Adrienne and I headed down to Venice when we heard that Betsy had changed course. We thought the Moreaus could use some help."

The General helped me sit up. I felt as if I had on a football helmet that was too small and then realized that all of my head above my ears was wrapped in tight layers of gauze. I got a bad headache once when a line drive hit me above the left eye while I was on the pitcher's mound, but that was a tiny baby compared to the one that hammered away at me now.

"He-Gene said Phil's mudpack probably kept you from bleeding out, probably saved your life," the General said. "Did you realize how deep the gash was?"

"No." I still dared not shake my head. The sequence of the day remained fuzzy. I felt a new pain in my left upper arm and began to rub it.

"He-Gene gave you a tetanus shot, a vitamin K shot to help

stop the bleeding, and a shot of morphine while you were out," the General said. "You probably shouldn't rub it."

"Where's my urn?" I put my arm on the back of the bench to stand.

"Relax. I've got it right here." The General moved the urn around to the front of the bench where I could see it. "You need to rest some more and get your feet under you . . . and I need to go over with you what I know about the plan so far."

He explained the plan in his newspaper way. Hurricane Betsy was on course to come ashore somewhere on the Louisiana coast in less than 24 hours. Venice was directly in its path if it kept the current track. The storm surge would come ahead of it. All shelters for a hundred miles above New Orleans would be full.

Captain Moreau agreed a good place to ride out the hurricane was on the General's barge in New Orleans with new and stronger tethers that they would have time to put in place. There was plenty of room for everyone on the barge. Highway 23, the evacuation route, was already crowded. Buster at the marina had called for an ambulance for me, but was told that the state police had stopped all southbound traffic, even emergency vehicles. The best time to head north would be after dark, which would allow time to pack and secure the Moreau house.

The more the General talked, the more my head cleared and the more the events of the day sorted themselves.

"As soon as you feel like it, we'll head over to the Captain's house," the General said.

"I'm ready now."

"I don't think so. I need to help He-Gene haul out his boat. When we're done, I'll come back and see how you feel."

"I can walk now," I protested.

"You have a long night ahead of you . . . and I don't think you realize how bad that gash was. I want you to lay back down and don't move."

The General's words came as an order, not a suggestion. I watched the clouds bang into one another and closed my eyes again. I wondered if I might hear my name again—Messenger— but all I heard was the confused river being pushed backward against itself.

Chapter 24

I opened my eyes to discover the shot that He-Gene had given me had made the throbbing in my head almost bearable. I had probably even slept a few minutes. Real sleep. Not passed-out sleep. I turned my head from side to side without wincing. The ramp area was noisy with boaters shouting and making ready to haul their rigs out of the river.

To make certain I was thinking straight, I sat up and imagined another manifest like Mr. Spiro had taught me: My shoes were somewhere at the bottom of the river. My billfold was in my back pocket, all the contents soaked. I felt for my car keys. They were wedged deep in my front pocket and safe. Dirty water sloshed around under the crystal of my wristwatch. The second-hand was not moving. Mr. Spiro's duffel bag was gone and my roll of twenty-dollar bills with it. My pants were torn and streaked with blood. The cut on my knee had stopped bleeding. My left bicep was red and ached from the shots, but aside from the drumming going on in my head, I found no other injuries.

I picked up the urn. It was dented in several places but the top was secure. Underneath the urn was Phil's fleur-de-lis bandana. I stuffed it in my back pocket.

The activity at the marina had grown more hectic. Buster, standing at the water's edge, shouted directions to boaters through his handheld loudspeaker.

The concrete ramp was wide enough to handle only two trailers at a time. Boat owners had to back their trailers into the river, leave the truck running, and go to their boat tied at the dock and drive it up on the trailer. Someone on the ramp would help the boater by getting into the truck and easing the trailer out of the water. Tie-downs were attached and made secure later in the marina parking lot. Everyone on the ramp and the docks moved with deadline urgency.

He-Gene and his packed-to-the-gills boat were next in line to haul out on the near side of the ramp. I picked up the urn and the General's shirt that had been my pillow, made sure of my footing, and headed toward the ramp, holding on to the dock railings for balance. The General backed He-Gene's truck down the ramp. My eyes focused enough to read the insignia on the door—*Crescent River Port Pilots' Association, Established 1908*. The trailer eased into the water until He-Gene, standing at the center console of the boat, raised his hand for the General to stop. The ramp was not as steep as the one near our cabin at Moon Lake, but the roiling river made the haul-out much more tricky.

On the far side of the ramp, another pickup—fire-engine red with enough lights for a Christmas tree—was in line for the haul-out. Jimmy LaBue stepped out of the driver's side. He left the truck idling. I watched closely. When it was his turn to begin the haul-out, he backed his tandem-wheel trailer into the water until only the top of its tires showed. He jumped out of the truck and hurried toward the end of the long dock. If Phil was with her father at the deep-water dock on the other side of the large marina, she would not have seen Jimmy LaBue and his boat. He-Gene and the General were busy with their own haul-out.

I waited for the bitter taste of bile to rise in my throat, but instead my anger turned itself into an unusual calmness, no doubt because of the shot that He-Gene had given me. The ribbed surface of the concrete ramp pricked my tender feet, helping me to sharpen my focus and find my balance. I handed the urn through the truck window to the General.

"Seems to me you're walking pretty good now," he said.

"Feeling fine. And here's your shirt. I'll be right back."

The deep rumble of the twin engines was unmistakable. Jimmy LaBue sat high on the back of the white upholstered seat for all to see, steering the *Crazy Eights* around the end of the dock toward his idling truck and trailer on the ramp. He disengaged the propellers and gunned the V-8 engines. The exhaust stacks were loud and designed to impress. All eyes were on Jimmy as he brought his fancy boat toward the trailer. I squinted to make out the knife sheath dangling from his belt.

A crosscurrent at the ramp required all boaters at take-out to concentrate on lining up with the trailer. Guided by the padded side rails, Jimmy LaBue eased the fiberglass hull of the *Crazy Eights* into its cradle on the trailer. He cut the engines after one last loud and aggressive rev of the sixteen cylinders.

The truck, standing tall on its oversized tires, hid me well until I walked around to the driver's door. A script was running in my head, which felt unusually focused, even covered with the tight layers of gauze. I shouted so everyone on the boat ramp could hear:

"Need some help, Jimmy LaBue?"

I slid into the idling truck. The floor shift was three times as tall as the one in my little car. The gearshift knob was made from a regulation billiard ball—the black eight. I pushed in the heavy clutch of Jimmy LaBue's truck, shifted into first gear, and pulled the trailer slowly ahead until the *Crazy Eights* was barely clear of the water. The side mirrors reflected the image of Jimmy LaBue standing in his boat, wildly jumping up and down, waving and shouting words I could not make out due to how loudly I gunned the truck's powerful engine.

My final thought on the ramp was that I should remember to thank my father for taking the time at Moon Lake to teach me about hauling out boats. I gripped the steering wheel, aimed the truck at the top of the ramp and popped the clutch.

The wetness of the ramp kept the tires from smoking until the spinning treads dried away the moisture. The wide tires then grabbed the ribbed concrete with violence. The truck fishtailed as it shot up the ramp. The trailer followed with corresponding movement. I looked in the rearview mirror to see the *Crazy Eights* hang and twist for a split second in midair and then crash to the ramp, throwing Jimmy LaBue backward on top of the hot exhaust pipes and then into the river. The heavy fiberglass hull cracked on the concrete with the sharp pop of a well-hit baseball. Shards of the fiberglass skin littered the ramp like a thousand broken light bulbs. One propeller drive collapsed under the weight of the boat and then the other. I stomped the brake pedal when the truck reached the top of the haul-out area.

My script was in my head again when I climbed out of the truck. Jimmy LaBue stood knee-deep in the river, splashing water on the exhaust-pipe burns on his arms and legs. His jeans were burned through in several places.

Again, the calmness.

"Sorry, Jimmy," I shouted. "College boys aren't very handy with trucks and boats."

Jimmy LaBue looked up at me. He pushed the wet black strands of his hair up away from his face with both hands. The way he always had his hair combed back, I didn't realize how long it was. Phil had mentioned his wild eyes on the river, but I doubt she had ever seen the way they looked at that moment. He yelled something I couldn't make out, but there was no doubt about the context. He came out of the water toward me, high stepping and grabbing for the knife on his belt. His feet made a sucking sound inside his red alligator boots.

The General and He-Gene had come up beside me.

"I see you two know each other," the General said to me in a calm voice.

"Not really," I answered.

Jimmy stopped halfway up the ramp, but continued his incoherent rant. Out of breath, he turned and limped back to inspect what was left of the *Crazy Eights* and to splash more river water on his burns.

I had a good idea that He-Gene's shot would keep me from passing out again, but I also felt my knees weren't going to hold me up much longer. When they buckled, the strong arms of the men on both sides caught me before I slumped to the ground.

* * *

Sitting between the two men on the short drive to the Moreaus' house, I felt something hard poking me in my side and looked down to see that He-Gene wore a black pistol clipped to his belt in a black holster with a gold badge attached.

"While you were passed out, Phil told us a little of what happened out there on the river," He-Gene said. "It's a good thing you got to Jimmy LaBue before Henri Moreau did."

The end was coming soon anyway for the young man from Cutoff, Louisiana, He-Gene told us. The Bureau of Narcotics had suspected LaBue of being a "sweeper" and had been trying to figure out the best way to deal with him. A sweeper, He-Gene explained, was somebody who used radio frequency identification devices to locate in-bound drug caches dropped from oceangoing freighters and smaller ships from the Caribbean and South America. The Bureau of Narcotics and Dangerous Drugs had known about Jimmy for some time but kept thinking the drug merchants would do everyone a favor and handle him on their own. Word was out that Jimmy had been stealing from the drug runners.

"I know he tried to hang around Phil some," He-Gene said. "I was glad to find out that she had stopped having anything to do with him. He was probably sweeping the river ahead of Betsy when you ran up on him."

The expensive saltwater reel. The custom-made cowboy boots. The practically new car he tried to give Phil. Dirty money had paid for them all. They didn't know half the story and I— the *bégayer boy*—wouldn't be the one to tell them.

The General chimed in. "One thing for sure. That boy is gonna have to get a broom and do some serious sweeping up one last time on the pieces of his boat you left him."

The two men chuckled. Not me. My hands and legs trembled.

"I'm impressed with how our young copyboy took over the situation." The General slapped me on my good knee. "What made you go after him like that?"

I shook my head. I wasn't sure of the answer, only that I had the urge and I didn't fight it. It just happened. The spur and the moment.

The only certainty I could hang on to in my cloudy memory of what had happened was the notion that if Jimmy LaBue was going to come after somebody, I wanted it to be me and not Philomene Moreau.

Chapter 25

Hurricane preparations had transformed the Moreau house from a comfortable family home into a wooden fort under siege.

Footlockers, ice chests, and old suitcases lined the second-floor porch. The Moreaus' newer truck and the General's pickup were backed in near the front stairs. Under the house, the heavy wooden tables had been turned on their sides to serve as a fence, corralling all manner of large and small outdoor items. Propane tanks had been gathered up and lashed to foundation posts.

Captain Moreau met us as we drove up. He looked at my bandaged head but didn't say anything to me.

"I told everyone we'd gather as soon as we all got here," the Captain said to He-Gene. "Before we go up, help me run this cable around the outside of the tables."

The General met Phil and Adrienne, each carrying a suitcase, coming down the stairs. I had to stand still once I got out of the truck to get my balance. Phil kept her eyes on me as the three talked. She put down the case she was carrying and came over.

"How's that head feeling?" She tucked in the bandage above my ears.

"It's b----etter. Still a little wobbly on my feet."

She smiled. "Not too wobbly, I hear, to take care of Jimmy LaBue and his fancy boat."

"Everything happened sort of fast."

Phil had changed into a tank top. For the first time I saw the bruises and scrapes on her neck and shoulder.

"Is that where I fell back into you? Are you okay?"

"A little bruised, but I'm not so sore that I couldn't catch me a swampy if I needed to." She took me by the arm and guided me to the stairs. "Take your hands out of your pockets and I'll steady you from behind. You need to go sit down."

I grabbed the stair rails quickly so Phil wouldn't see my hands shaking.

★ ★ ★

No one interrupted Captain Moreau as he laid out the evacuation plan like it was something he did every morning at the breakfast table over sausage sandwiches. His veteran-river-pilot voice was calm and direct.

He and the General would take the *Rooster* upriver to the barge. He-Gene needed to leave for the Federal Building in New Orleans as soon as they could get a waterproof tarp over his boat and its contents. She-Gene and Adrienne would drive the two pickups. The two brothers would ride with Adrienne in her truck and the two sisters with their mother. Since Phil knew Highway 23, she would drive my car and I would ride with her.

The idea of riding with Phil all the way to New Orleans appealed to me.

The Captain and the General would leave on the *Rooster* as soon as it could be loaded and the house secured. They would need the extra time in New Orleans to add heavier mooring lines to the barge and put the *Rooster* in a spiderweb rig to ride out the storm surge.

All gasoline stations this side of New Orleans would be out of fuel. Everyone should top off their tanks from the gasoline cans under the house. The traffic on Highway 23 might thin out a little an hour or so after dark. Leaving then should get everyone to the barge by sun-up and at least eight hours ahead of the brunt of the hurricane.

"Long night ahead for everybody, but we can sleep tomorrow," the Captain said. "Any questions?"

Phil had been silent.

"Does this Betsy have the makings of a bad one, Daddy?"

"Coming back in this morning on the *Rooster*, I saw deer and wild pigs moving to higher ground and gators passing up good meals right in front of them. That speaks to me more than the weather forecasters."

Captain Moreau stood. He had a final word for the group. "When I was piloting years ago I talked to a freighter captain who lost half his crew to the first Hurricane Betsy that hit the Caribbean in '56. We won't trifle with another hurricane with that name."

He-Gene turned to She-Gene. "If you haven't packed the coffee pot yet, Sister, I've got a Thermos I could fill. And can I talk to you outside, Henri?" The two men went out the front door.

Sounding much like her husband, She-Gene took over and began her own set of instructions to the family.

"You little ones get a trash can each for your clothes and belongings. Daddy has them cleaned out and drying under the house. Miss Adrienne will help you pack them. Phil, the best of the kitchen can go in our two big washtubs."

I stood with the help of a chair. "What can I do?"

"Henri asked me to pack up the radio," the General said. "You can help me with that if you feel like it."

"Good to go." My head throbbed no matter if I was standing or sitting. I had thought about asking He-Gene for another pain shot before he left but I wanted to stay as clearheaded as I could. I kept going over the events of the day to remind myself where I had been, where I was at present, and where I was headed.

Everyone—the Moreau family, the General, Adrienne—moved in that no-nonsense manner like a newsroom on deadline. Short conversations took place on the run and were all about the business at hand. Outside, Captain Moreau wrestled sheets of plywood up the stairs in the gradually increasing wind gusts. He nailed them in place over the windows. It was the same plywood that the dancers had done the Cajun two-step on just the night before at the *fais do-do*.

"Before we unplug, we'll give the Coast Guard weather another listen," the General said.

Betsy's eye had passed just south of Miami with sustained winds of 140 miles an hour. The Overseas Highway and its 42 bridges to Key West were underwater. The Category 3 hurricane was picking up intensity again as it headed on a northwesterly track in the warmer waters of the gulf.

The General switched off the shortwave radio. "Those are our marching orders," he said to everyone.

The newsroom had begun to feel like a family to me in

Memphis, and I felt the same thing in Venice, Louisiana, in the Moreau house that was calmly going about the business of preparing for the worst.

★ ★ ★

The rain came out of the south, light but steady. Phil drove to the marina with the General and the Captain seated on the lowered tailgate of the truck that was packed with food from the Moreaus' freezer and refrigerator. I had discarded my bloody clothes at the house and changed into a pair of clean shorts and a shirt that belonged to the Captain. I also had on a pair of his old deck shoes, which were at least two sizes too big for me.

Most of the charter boats had already left their slips for safer harbors. Other boat owners, gambling that Venice would escape a direct hit, simply added extra dock lines. Phil explained how a spiderweb rig worked, but I had trouble following her. I had the sense she was talking to me to see if my brain was working the way it should, and I couldn't be sure it was.

Captain Moreau jumped off the tailgate before the truck stopped. It seemed to be a family trait. He came to the passenger-side window.

"The office saved me some block ice," he said. "You two run over there in the truck and bring me what they have."

Captain Moreau looked at me. "You probably need to let your folks up in Memphis know you're okay."

"I should." My answer was on the sheepish side. The thought of contacting my parents had not crossed my mind for some reason. They would have read about the hurricane in the afternoon's *Press-Scimitar*.

"Tell Buster to let Vic have a long-distance line and to put it on my account. If the phone lines are tied up, see if they can still send a telegram."

Phil backed the truck up to the marina icehouse. Buster met her and then came over to my window.

"I don't knowed what you and Jimmy LaBue had going on, but I'll say you did what most of us been wantin' to do for a long time," Buster said. "Might have something to do with that bandage on your head, mightn't it?"

I nodded. "Long story."

"All the long-distance lines are jammed. You want me to try to do you a Western Union?"

I had read a few telegrams that came to my father but had never gone about the process of sending one. I liked how they were written with the extra words left out.

In the office, Buster gave me a Western Union pad and a pencil. After I filled in my home address and composed my message, he converted it to telegram talk and read it back to me.

"I'm safe. STOP. Back tomorrow PM. STOP. Lots to tell. STOP. Victor. END."

"How's that sound?" Buster asked.

I liked the short words and the no-fooling-around of the sentences, but something was missing.

"Can you add 'love' in front of Victor?"

"You bet. I'll get it off straightway to Memphis. And listen, you come back to see us if'n old Betsy girl don't blow us away. From what I hear, Jimmy LaBue ain't gonna be round no more to bother nobody." Buster laughed. "Hooo-boy. I bet he feels like he done been crotch bit by an alligator, sure."

★ ★ ★

203

Phil scurried around the *Rooster Tale*, helping prepare it for the night trip upriver to New Orleans. The Captain asked her to build a line-and-spring rig so their small boat could be towed safely behind the *Rooster*. Still not steady enough on my feet to be walking on a dock, I sat on a nearby bench in the drizzle and watched her nimble fingers work.

I wanted to make small talk.

"Think you could teach me to tie kn----ots like that?"

"You mean they won't teach knot-tying in that fancy college of yours?" She smiled but never took her eyes off her work. "You may be smart with books, but I don't know if you college boys can handle a double running bowline."

I collected Phil's sassy talk like I had collected Mr. Spiro's grand words. I wanted to have them close to me when it came time for me to leave.

The lights on the wharf came on. Captain Moreau jumped to the dock near me with a light windbreaker in his hand.

"Take this," he said. "I don't know if we'll have a chance to talk in New Orleans, but I'd like for you to come down to visit us again and we'll make it a point to see you don't get so banged up next time."

He stuck out his weathered hand. "I admire your standing up to that no-count LaBue boy. Gene will see that young scoundrel gets what's due him. Most people think my brother-in-law just sits in Pilottown and talks on his squawk box all day, but nothing goes on out there on the river that he doesn't know about."

I fumbled to zip the jacket but couldn't line up the two halves of the zipper. The Captain fastened it for me.

"By the way, I put the urn in the front seat of your car,"

he said. "No sense to lose track of it now after all you've been through with it."

Captain Moreau stepped on the *Rooster*, hauled in the gangplank, and climbed into the pilot's chair on the main deck. The *Rooster's* engines rumbled to life.

"How's your fuel?" Phil shouted to her father.

"Topped it off as soon as we came in."

Phil looked at me over her shoulder. "Should have known better than to ask."

"Throw the tow line to the General when I clear the dock," the Captain ordered. "And make sure everybody gets out of here on time. I'm puttin' you in charge."

"Aye, aye, Captain," Phil said.

We watched the *Rooster Tale* pull out of the dock area and turn north with the wind into the main channel. The General used a bright spotlight to scan the dark river ahead. The little boat, the one that Phil and I survived the river in, followed the *Rooster* like a puppy on a leash.

The rain picked up.

"That jacket needs to go over your head to keep your bandage dry," Phil said. "You heard the Captain. I'm in charge."

"Okay . . . I mean . . . aye, aye, Captain."

Phil tied the windbreaker around my head, took my arm, and helped me to the truck.

"Probably no sense in telling you this now, but out there on the river I could see straight into the white of your skull bone." She tightened her grip on my arm. "Coming back up the river, I never prayed so hard to my Jesus in all my born days."

"How d----id you know to make that mudpack for my head?"

"The bottom mud in the river is about as clean as mud gets . . . and the old-timers say it has healing properties. That's what we use to patch up dogs when they get in fights or when gators get hold of them." She smiled at me. "Woof, woof."

Riding in the truck, I tested myself again to come up with a manifest of my condition and emotions. My head in the tight bandage ached. I was unable to walk without wobbling in shoes that didn't fit. A hurricane was bearing down on me. I was happy to be sitting beside Phil. Juxtaposition.

★ ★ ★

Only 24 hours before, the Moreau house had been a place of music, dance, delicious food, and laughter.

Through the truck's windshield wipers, I saw the sad boarded-up windows and the radio antenna lying flat on the porch. Phil's old motorbike and the family's five bicycles were lashed to the porch railing. The Moreaus' oldest truck was parked next to the concrete pad under the house, standing a lonely guard.

Footlockers and garbage cans with lids roped down filled the bed of Adrienne's truck. More containers were on the ground waiting to be packed in the pickup that Phil and I drove up in.

"I'll load the truck and then go top off your gas tank." Phil looked over her shoulder as she backed in near the stairs.

"I'll be h----appy to pay you for the gas."

Phil turned toward me and leaned her head on the steering wheel.

"Lord, trust my words. I've never met anyone like my man from Memphis . . . and I know I never will again."

I was happy with the "man from Memphis" part, but the "never will again" didn't sound right to me. She was out of the truck and running while I was trying to make sense of what she meant by "never will again."

Adrienne came down the stairs, her knees banging against a garbage can.

"Let me help with that." I stepped out of the truck.

"You stay where you are. The General filled me in on the day you've had."

I leaned against the tailgate.

"Seems like you've made the most out of your trip to Louisiana," Adrienne said. "The General and I wondered what you were going to think of Phil if you got the chance to meet her."

Adrienne didn't ask a question, but she waited for an answer anyway.

"I guess I can say I've n----ever met anyone like her." No way was I going to add "and never will again."

Phil held my gym bag and yelled down to me from the porch.

"Do you have your car keys on you?"

I pulled the keys from my front pocket and dangled them. She ran down the stairs and grabbed them out of my hand.

"Show me how to crank this little doodle-bug of yours."

Before I could get to the car, she had it started and in reverse. She backed it around to the side of the house near some red gasoline cans.

I went to the passenger side and saw the urn in the seat. When I reached down to try to pick up the typewriter from the floorboard, I lost my balance. I turned, leaned against the car, and eased myself to the ground.

"Let me do that." Phil put down her gasoline can. "Tell me where you want everything."

"P----ut the typewriter in the trunk with my gym bag. The urn can go under my legs."

"I'm taking you up to lie down until we get everything ready to go. You're wobbling like you just drank a six-pack of Dixie."

"At least I'm not talking f----unny."

Phil didn't smile until my smile gave her the okay. We were getting to understand each other like that.

Chapter 26

Highway 23 at ten o'clock at night was as busy as the streets of downtown New Orleans at rush hour.

In addition to cars and trucks, the road was clogged with motor homes, livestock trailers, and farmers on tractors trying to get their machines to higher ground. Cars towed open trailers heaped high with any household items that wouldn't be ruined by the rain. Some tried to cover their pickup-truck beds with tarps, but most of those ended up flapping like sheets on a clothesline and letting the rain in anyway.

We began the drive to New Orleans in a convoy. Adrienne led in her truck with the two boys. Phil and I followed in my car. She-Gene and the girls brought up the rear, but the Louisiana State Police at some point turned both lanes into a one-way heading north and we got separated. Windshield wipers weren't helping much against the sheets of sideways rain.

My friends back home found my car hard to drive with its tight clutch and quick steering, but Phil handled it without a problem. The traffic was so heavy that we never got above thirty miles an hour. I had remembered to ask She-Gene for some towels before we left, knowing that the roof seal at the top of the windshield and the sliding windows would leak if the wind blew a certain way.

"If this traffic keeps up like this, it might be after daylight before we get to the barge," Phil said.

"I'll still have enough time to drive to Memphis and get some sleep before I have to go to work."

"You won't have time to do that much sleeping. Traffic will be just as bad on the north side of New Orleans. You need to hunker down with us on the barge."

"My friend says sleep is highly overrated." I told Phil about Charlie Roker and the story of how he helped me trick the funeral home into letting me have the urn.

"You seem more excited about getting back to your friends at the newspaper than starting college."

"I guess I am. My I-Powers were working well when I decided to keep my job at the newspaper."

She down-shifted as the truck in front of us slowed to a crawl.

"So, what's this I-Powers thing, pray tell? Sounds like voodoo-who-doo to me. You said you'd tell me about it."

"I will, but you have to p----romise not to say I'm crazy. I tried to explain it to my friend Art once and he told me I had finally gone completely off my rocker."

I lined up my words to tell Phil as best I could about Mr. Spiro's theory of the twin I-Powers: intellect and intuition.

"Humans possess two p----owers in separate parts of their

brains," I said. "Mr. Spiro explained it to me one afternoon on his porch swing that intellect was the product of experience and reasoning on the left side of the brain. Intellect handled things as they were. Intuition on the right side of the brain had to do more with feelings and thinking about the future. Intuition was in charge of how things could be."

I was concentrating so hard on how to explain all this to Phil that I almost forgot to stutter, but the sputtering never left me for very long.

"Mr. Spiro said the best d----ecisions are made when the two sides of the b----rain worked together as a team. Wh----en one of the I-Powers got ahead of the other, a p----erson was more likely to make a bad decision."

I wasn't sure if Phil understood anything I had explained.

"So, see if I have this right," she said. "When you started swimming after the urn and not to the shore, you were only using half your brain. The intuition side."

"That's exactly it." Phil could handle a lot more than complicated knots. "But I got lucky and it turned out okay, thanks to you."

"And when you yanked the *Crazy Eights* out from under Jimmy LaBue, you were only using half your brain again."

I had to think a minute.

"We might could say I wasn't using much of my brain on either side on that one." I touched my bandaged head. "I can't exactly tell what made me do that. The shot that He-Gene gave me might have had something to do with it."

Phil took my hand and put it on the gearshift under hers.

"What do you think about what Daddy said this morning about me being afraid to leave home?"

VINCE VAWTER

Questions that put me on the spot usually threw me for a loop, but part of me had been expecting this one, and I was glad Phil wanted to talk to me about it. I had a good answer ready for her.

"I think that those who love and respect you the most are the ones who tell you the things you don't want to hear."

There wasn't much stuttering in my answer. For once, words came out the way and in the order I heard them in my head. Phil looked at the road through the rain and windshield wipers. I had another thought saved up for her.

"Like I was glad that you told me the meaning of the word that Jimmy LaBue called me. I knew what it meant from the way he said it, but I wanted you to translate it for me to my face. It let me know you had confidence that I could handle it."

Traffic in both lanes heading north came to a complete stop. A state police car with its siren blaring came by on the shoulder, spraying mud on my side of the car. We inched ahead and saw a family standing by an old trailer with a broken axle.

Phil finally spoke.

"So, do you think that Daddy is right about me being afraid to leave home? I can't help it that I like to be out on the *Rooster* and the water. And, if you noticed, I'm a pretty good hand. I can't see myself stuck inside in a classroom or some office."

She was going at a good clip and I could feel how hard it was for her to talk about herself. I didn't interrupt.

"My friends leave for college or a job in the city and then come back home even more confused about what they want to do with their lives. They don't seem to me to be any smarter or any happier than when they left."

"I can't tell you what you should do, only that you need to

m----ake sure you pay attention to both your I-Powers."

"My brain may not be split up like Mr. Spiro talked about."

No need to get into that argument, so I brought it back to me.

"At first, it was hard for me to think about giving up playing baseball because I thought I liked it so much. Even though I was good at it, one part of me said I played it for the wrong reason."

"And what reason is that?"

"I played it to prove I was good at something and to make up for not being able to t----alk like everybody else." Telling a truth out loud was harder than just thinking the truth. "That was the wrong reason for p----laying. When I thought about it like that, I didn't enjoy baseball as much."

The focused expression on Phil's face told me she had shut down. She was thinking hard about something, but I had no idea what. I had one more thought for her that was risky.

"I told She-Gene this morning that I thought V----enice was a great place. I couldn't imagine anything more fun than a *fais do-do* or chasing swamp rabbits, but I was using only one side of my b----rain. Your mother made me see that it's a hard life on the river. I see families with their lives p----acked in an old trailer and trying to outrun a hurricane."

She came back at me hard and fast, the way she ran down rabbits and danced the two-step. "So, you're saying I should leave. Leave everything that I love. Is that what you're saying?"

I wanted to make sure my words didn't sound hollow. "No. I'm saying open yourself up to everything inside you before you make a decision. Just like you did when you decided you needed to get away from Jimmy LaBue."

Silence.

I squeezed Mr. Spiro's urn on the floorboard between my feet.

* * *

The pace of the traffic was monotonous. Phil yawned. I dared not. Yawning made the throbbing in my head worse.

"I see a place to pull off up ahead," Phil said. "A little sleep would do us more good than this stop-and-go traffic. Maybe it will clear out a little if we give it a rest."

She turned off the engine, folded her arms, and leaned back in her seat. As tired as I was, sleeping upright was out of the question. I turned on the faint dash light and pulled out my billfold to dry out the contents. I spread out my driver's license, library card, draft card, and taped-together dollar bill on top of the dashboard. Mr. Spiro's obituary clipping on the thin newsprint was ruined, as were two photos of girls in my senior class. I would be able to clip another obit when I got back to the newspaper, and the two photos didn't seem too important now.

I closed my eyes and listened to the rain beat on the canvas roof. The throbbing in my head eased slightly. My condition improved again when Phil wadded towels into a pillow on my shoulder and rested her head there. Mr. Spiro would have liked Philomene Moreau, and not because she could tie sailors' knots and handle a boat. She was a good thinker and no doubt already knew the answer to Mr. Spiro's riddle about if it's best to know where you have been, where you are, or where you are going.

"I think knowing where you are is the most important," I told Mr. Spiro one afternoon on his porch swing. "Because it's the best clue to where you have been and to where you might be headed."

"Excellent reasoning, Messenger," Mr. Spiro said. "You view the past, you sense the future, but you live in the present, the perfect here and now."

I felt Phil's even breaths as she slept in the perfection of the present.

★ ★ ★

A tapping on the driver's-side window woke me. Even with the wind howling, the rain pelting the canvas top, and the constant traffic, I had fallen asleep. Phil slid open her window.

"State police, ma'am. Everything okay?" The officer wore a yellow raincoat with a hood instead of the usual wide-brimmed hat.

"We're good. Just pulled over to get a little rest," Phil said to the officer. "Been going hard all day, same as everybody else, sure."

"Probably need to move on before the daylight traffic picks up. Are y'all headed all the way back to Tennessee?"

"We've got shelter in New Orleans if we can ever get there." Phil glanced at me. "We'll see after that."

I looked at my watch and remembered it was a victim of the river.

"Wh----at time is it?" I asked the officer.

"Half-past four."

We had been off the road for maybe two hours, but I felt like I had a full night's sleep. I could tell my head was getting back to somewhere near normal. Sleep was not overrated when you had a head that needed to heal.

"What's the latest on Betsy?" Phil asked.

"Still taking dead aim at New Orleans. Her eye's likely to hit the lower delta early afternoon and the city by nightfall. Storm surge is already showing up at Venice and Boothville."

"I need to get out and take a *pissotiere*," she said to the officer. "Then we'll be on our way."

The officer laughed.

"Yes, ma'am," he said. "I can tell now you're not from Tennessee."

Phil didn't surprise me much anymore with what she said or how she said it. I handed her one of the towels. I draped the other one over the urn under my legs.

"How's Mr. Spiro?" she asked.

I patted the top of the urn. "Safe and sound."

Resting on the couch at the Moreau house before we left, I started working on a new plan for Mr. Spiro, even though I wasn't sure my head was up to it. The more I considered the plan, however, the more sense it made. Phil once again could help me carry out what I had in mind.

She spread the towel on the seat when she got back to the car.

"Remind me how close to the General's b----arge is the big b----ridge over the river," I said.

"Not too far. Are you thinking about something I should know about?"

"The b----ridge is where I want to spread Mr. Spiro's ashes."

"What about the Southwest Pass? What about our mullet? I was thinking you could come back when things calmed down and we could finish what we started." The depth of her disappointment surprised me. "I was even going to ask you if you wanted me to keep Mr. Spiro until you could get back down here. You'd trust me, wouldn't you?"

"Of course, but—"

Phil interrupted. "The bridge in New Orleans is a hundred miles from the gulf. You know it's nowhere near the mouth of the river you've been trying to find."

"Let's get b----ack on the highway," I said. "This is going to take some time to talk out."

I would explain my new way of thinking to Phil at the same time I explained it to myself.

I missed Mr. Spiro the most when I had something complicated that needed thinking through, almost like warming up to pitch a ballgame without anyone to catch me.

I was counting on Phil to understand my new thoughts about the mouth of the river as they came unrehearsed out of my own mouth.

"The General gave me the first clue when he asked if Mr. Spiro's last request might actually be a gift . . . in disguise . . . for me . . . and the more I moved that around in my head, the more it sounded like something that Mr. Spiro would do."

Phil focused on the red taillights ahead without saying anything. She didn't have the patience to wait for a car to stop before she jumped out, but she had patience with me when she saw that I needed it. I continued.

"I had in mind an X on a chart when I first started thinking about how to keep my promise. I thought the Mouth of the Mississippi River would be like an intersection of two roads on a map. But the mouth is wherever you convince yourself it is. It's not the same for everybody."

"Keep going," Phil said.

"Your father found it with the dancing mullets. Mile Marker 0 at Head of Passes was good enough for the General, and then I remembered you said that the mouth of a river is like the end of a rainbow because it has to end somewhere but no one can be sure where it is."

Phil pulled out of the traffic and onto the shoulder of the highway. She left the engine running.

"So you've convinced yourself that the bridge in New Orleans is the location of the mouth of the Mississippi River?"

"New Orleans is where Mr. Spiro was born," I said. "The river will take his ashes to where they belong."

Phil wiped the fog of our breaths from the inside of the windshield with a towel.

"I guess I can understand that, but I don't understand about the gift from Mr. Spiro. What's the gift?"

My thoughts cleared like the windshield without the fog.

"The journey he sent me on to spread his ashes was his gift to me," I said. "It wasn't about him. It was about me."

I glanced at Phil. She stared straight ahead.

"And it turns out that you're my gift. Your family is my gift. The General and Adrienne are my gifts. Even though I hate to say it, Jimmy LaBue is my gift. Mr. Spiro gave me the gift of seeing things on my own, meeting new people, experiencing new feelings."

Phil looked to her left and eased back onto the highway. I waited for her to say something. Anything.

A little ways up the road, Phil took my hand again and placed it on the gearshift under hers.

"Thank you, Mr. Spiro," she said.

Chapter 27

We drove in silence in the pounding rain and in traffic that got heavier the closer we got to New Orleans. I didn't know if the lack of conversation was due to the noise of the storm and the heavy traffic or if we were each thinking our own hard thoughts. Morning light fought its way through banks of dark clouds fighting for their space. Highway 23 dumped us into the south suburbs of New Orleans. Phil maneuvered the little car through the traffic and rain-slick streets with the same confidence and skill that she dodged logs in the river.

"The bridge is going to be crowded and dangerous," she said. "How do you have in mind that we should go about this?"

The approach to the bridge was lengthy with a gradual rise. It would be impossible to park on the bridge.

"Can we p----ark somewhere and walk out to the middle?"

"I'm game if you think you're steady enough on your feet."

Phil pulled the car over the curb and parked on the sidewalk. "Nobody's going to be walking here," she said, "except for two crazy people I know."

"Y----ou mean two *couyons*?" I was getting good at making Phil smile.

The tape sealing the top to the urn, even after all it had been through, had not lost its holding power. I picked at the sticky goo without success. The wind blew so hard that the sliding window on my side inched open on its own.

"You don't have any fingernails," Phil said. "Let me try."

She worked on the top of the urn with the nimble fingers that tied sailor's knots and fine-tuned outboard engines. After running her fingernail under the top, she twisted off the brass cap and handed me the urn.

I looked inside. "It's not even half full," I said.

"Ashes to ashes. Dust to dust. Genesis 3:19," Phil said.

She was right. I carried the whole of Mr. Spiro inside me.

I unzipped the windbreaker Captain Moreau had given me and offered it to Phil.

"Rain's not going to melt me. I'll put it over your bandage again." She wrapped the windbreaker around my head, twisted and tied it. She put a towel over her head.

"Now, don't we make a *couple heureux*?" Phil said. "A happy couple." She was joking but I didn't want her words to be a joke.

"Yes, if you want to know the truth, I think we do." She looked at me and smiled. I was getting better at putting some meaning into my sentences.

I walked with one arm clutching the urn and the other arm

around Phil to steady myself against the gusts that blew the rain sideways. When we got to the bridge, we walked in single file holding on to the railing.

Phil shouted over the whipping wind: "You said that even Jimmy LaBue was your gift."

"Right."

"Then Hurricane Betsy must be your gift, too."

"Right again."

"We just need to make sure this gift of yours doesn't blow our butts back down into the river." Phil caught on quickly to new concepts.

A continuous stream of cars and trucks crawled across the bridge. The Mississippi River was a world of its own far below us, a tangle of violent swirls and white froth.

I handed the urn to Phil. "Hold it with both hands." She braced herself against a steel girder. I took off the top with one hand and reached into the urn with the other.

Mr. Spiro gave his four words to me that summer in 1959 when I was his paperboy for a month. I'd had six years to think about the four words and how they fit into Mr. Spiro's way of life that he called the "Quartering of the Soul."

I took out a handful of ashes. I shouted the first word as I gave part of Mr. Spiro to the howling wind.

"STUDENT!"

As the ashes were carried away by the storm's rage, I thought about the time I talked to Mr. Spiro about going to college and what I might study so I could make sure I got out in four years and didn't get in trouble with the draft board. He gave me one of his lectures where his eyes didn't blink. He said that a student is measured by grades and degrees to a fault. There should be no end to learning, no sense of a destination reached, or a cup that is full, he said. Learning is like breathing. If we stop, a part of our soul withers.

I reached into the urn for the next handful. I threw the ashes as far as the wind would let me.

"SERVANT!"

I recalled the day I found Mr. Spiro fixing a lady neighbor's broken-down fence. I pulled nails out of the old boards for him and helped him scrape off flaking paint. He worked an entire week on the fence. I came back to help him paint it on the last day and asked if his neighbor was going to pay him for all the hard work he had done. "We are the ones who owe the debt, Messenger. Helping others is our balance due for the privilege of life." He did admit that he had accepted a homemade cherry pie from his neighbor and that we would be enjoying those sweet proceeds as soon as we could clean all the paint off our hands.

Once again, I shouted into the rain and wind.

"SELLER!"

When I told Mr. Spiro I had gotten the copyboy job, he explained it was a good way to trade the one commodity I could call my own—time. "You must make your own way in the world by selling your time," he said, "but be careful not to sell yourself out." I asked him if maybe that is what my father was doing by working so long and hard and not having time for anything else. A good question, he allowed. Had I raised the subject with my father? No. Like the many other subjects I had been too afraid to raise with him.

I shouted the last word the loudest of all as I rose on my toes to throw the handful of ashes.

"SEEKER!"

One time when Mr. Spiro and I sat and watched the river from our favorite spot, I asked him what it must have been like for the first explorers to come down the Mississippi River in a boat without having any idea what was in store for them. He came back with questions that were meant to knock me for a loop. Do you know where you are headed now? Have you sought any directions for the path you find yourself on? Have you considered who put you here and how you arrived at the place you are now? As usual, I shook my head. "As you go about the business of living, Messenger, seek to understand a higher power that exists in a realm that is above us. To pretend there is nothing beyond the finite dimension of man is the highest form of conceit, ego, and contempt for life."

Even though the wind cut into us on the bridge and the rain stung our faces, Phil and I looked out over the river for a moment.

I had put in plenty of time thinking about the four words. I was confident I finally understood the Quartering of the Soul and that the real trick is to keep the four parts equal in your life like they are equal on the four pieces of the taped-together dollar bill. If one of the four parts becomes more important than the others, you'll lose your balance and eventually lose your way.

Phil and I once again looked down at the swirling river, at the water that wanted to go to the gulf but was being held back by the storm surge of the advancing hurricane. I put my arm around Phil and felt my own storm surge of happiness and the sense I had fulfilled my promise to Mr. Spiro.

★ ★ ★

I gripped the railing hand-over-hand as we made our way off the bridge. A gust of wind whipped the windbreaker off my bandaged head. It fluttered like a runaway kite out over the river.

I tripped when one of Captain Moreau's shoes that were too large for me came off.

"Kick the other one off and let's get out of here," Phil yelled above the wind.

When we got near the car, I told Phil I wanted to drive to the barge to make sure I could handle the four hundred miles back to Memphis.

Safe inside the car, Phil dried her hands on a towel. She shook the brass container and then twisted off the top.

"There's something else in the bottom," she said.

"I kn----ow some ashes are left. I'm going to keep those in the urn on my bookshelves."

"No. There's something else. It looks like a dollar bill with some writing on it."

I reached into the urn.

I read the words on the new dollar bill in Mr. Spiro's familiar handwriting. I handed it to Phil. She nodded, either that she agreed with what was written or that she understood the meaning of the words. Neither of us had anything to say.

The traffic had backed up on the bridge access. The honking got louder. We needed to get going, but I couldn't make my hand reach for the switch. I found myself not wanting to leave the bridge and Mr. Spiro.

The tears were not too far away.

"It's okay," Phil said.

But then the spur was followed by the moment, and I decided this final tribute on the bridge to a life well lived was not a place for tears. I had kept my promise and that was a victory that didn't need tears.

I smiled at Phil and turned the key.

Chapter 28

Phil directed me through the tight streets. Homeowners struggled to maneuver sheets of plywood over windows and doors like Captain Moreau had done in Venice. Small boats were tied down on front porches in case a last-minute escape was called for. People who lived near the river went about their hurricane preparation with a calmness they had earned through experience.

I slammed on the brakes when a metal gas station sign cartwheeled across the street in front of us.

"If you're still bound and determined not to stay safe with us on the barge, at least you'll have a good tailwind back to Memphis," Phil said.

I could never describe to Phil how much I wanted to stay with her and to outlast the hurricane together, but the journey that Mr. Spiro had sent me on was all about helping me grow, and that part of me said it was time for me to head back home.

I recognized the two familiar pickup trucks as we neared the barge's mooring at the riverbank. The General had opened a larger hatch on the far end of the barge and was handing down one of the garbage cans the Moreau family had packed.

"One last time." Phil twisted in her seat to look at me. "There's plenty of room on the barge and it's the safest place. You know the General and Adrienne will want you to stay."

"I have to be at work at four o'clock in the morning and I'm anxious to start taking care of some things."

Phil said, "You're *entêté*, Victor Vollmer the Third."

Instead of requesting a translation, I just asked with my look.

"Stubborn. Pigheaded. Take your pick."

She leaned over and kissed me on the cheek. She might have considered it a "sissy little Memphis kiss," but that's the kind it needed to be. Phil was letting me go.

She was out of the car and running as usual, shouting against the wind.

"At least come say goodbye to everybody."

I watched her skip across a longer gangplank that had been installed on the barge already riding higher in the river with the first of the storm surge. She had said my last name, and I had no idea how she knew I was "the Third." When would I learn not to underestimate the girl who could run down a swamp rabbit and save my life with river mud?

The barge's mooring lines had been lengthened and the half-round metal covers had been moved into place and locked down to protect the glass skylights. The *Rooster Tale* rocked nearby in a complicated web of lines attached to cleats on the barge and iron rings on the riverbank. The fly bridge was buttoned up in its canvas shroud. A dim light was on inside the cabin.

All the Moreau family members, except for the Captain, were inside the barge. The four youngest Moreaus sat at the big table, gnawing on giant sandwiches. Adrienne and She-Gene had stuffed the refrigerator and freezer with the food brought upriver in the *Rooster's* large ice compartment. Lights flickered.

"How's your head?" the General asked as I backed down the ladder to the barge's floor.

"Much better," I said. "I can m----ake it to Memphis without any problems."

"Plenty of fuel in the generator here," the General said. "We're in good shape if we lose shore power. It would be best to ride it out here with us."

"I need to head home," I said.

"Come over here under the light," the General ordered. "I want to make sure your bandage is holding."

The General turned me around several times.

"I need you to look me square in the eyes and tell me you are up to making the drive to Memphis."

I mustered all my conviction. "I need to get home . . . I'll be fine."

"Okay," he said. "I'm not going to press it. If Philomene couldn't convince you, I'm sure I wouldn't have much luck." He winked at Adrienne.

Phil dug through a suitcase. She pulled on an old windbreaker and handed one to me that had a hood attached. She turned to her mother.

"Daddy must be on the *Rooster*."

"Yes," She-Gene said. "He wants you to come help him adjust the lines after you get a bite to eat."

"Not hungry," Phil said, reaching for the ladder to the deck.

"Aren't you going to tell Vic goodbye?" She-Gene called out.

"Already did, Momma. He'll be back to see us, sure. I *garanti*." I took the heavier accent to be for my benefit. I know that was true of her smile and wink.

Phil climbed the ladder and vaulted through the hatch into the rain and wind in one fluid motion. Strong. Stronger. Strongest.

I was going to use something that Mr. Spiro told me once to keep from feeling so bad about leaving Phil. A year or so after Mam had left us to go back to Coldwater, I was complaining to him about how much I missed her. I went on and on about it. He listened without saying anything and then when I was finished, he lowered the boom on me with just one sentence: "Whether bad or good, Messenger, we always ARE who we WERE."

I had to think for weeks about what he meant by that and then I figured it out. Don't let anything take away from the past, especially the good. If I thought about it like that, Phil would always be with me.

The General gave me quick directions on the best way out of the city. He said I should take the extra time to go around Lake Pontchartrain since the causeway likely would be closed. I could pick up Highway 51 North on the west side of the lake, he said.

My goodbyes were quick.

"Here's a lunch I packed for you," Adrienne said. "Wish I had some beignets for you." She kissed me on the cheek. She-Gene hugged me.

"Tell the Rocket to get his butt down here before too long," the General said. "The bartenders at La Casa de Los Marinos have been asking about him." He shook my hand.

Halfway up the ladder, I turned to the General.

"I have something in my car I need you to give Phil," I said. "I'll be right back."

I opened the trunk for my gym bag and remembered I didn't have a pencil or paper. I hauled out my typewriter. Inside the car as the rain beat down on the canvas top, I carefully tore out the title page from *The Old Man and the Sea*, pushed the seat back as far as it would go, and rested the typewriter against the steering wheel at an awkward angle. I began typing.

Dear Phil,
    I wanted to give you something and this book is all I have. You will get more out of it anyway since you know a lot about the sea. You'll find out there's more to it than just a story about catching a big fish, and you'll read about how the old man dreamed about the lions on the beach. That's what I wanted to dream about until I met you. Now I only want to dream about the mullet dancing.
    You are my best gift.

Love,
Sporty Boy

I returned the page to the book and went back to give it to the General.

Mr. Spiro was right. We don't own books. We borrow them and pass them on. What we own is what the books leave inside of us.

★ ★ ★

Both the rain and traffic were heavy on Highway 51 North all the way to Jackson, Mississippi. The needle on my gas gauge rested on empty when I pulled into the familiar Esso station.

Fred, in his uniform, and an older man were hunched over a radio near the cash register. Fred recognized me.

"Well, if it ain't Mr. Businessman and his typewriter. Looks like you had yourself quite a time in New Orleans without me."

I had forgotten about the bandage on my head. Fred continued to look me up and down. I held my typewriter in my hands in front of me

"Man, you didn't even make it back with your shoes. I've lost a bunch of stuff in New Orleans, but I ain't never come back without my shoes." We both smiled. I was glad to see Fred again.

"I'm out of g----as and need to get to Memphis, but I lost my extra money." The two men stared at me. "Could I trade this ty----pewriter for a t----ank of gas?"

I got the feeling they had never had an offer resembling mine.

The older man spoke. "We're just fixin' to shut off the pumps and lock up before the winds hit. We don't have much call round here for typewriters."

"Put it on the counter," Fred said. He tore off a shop ticket from a pad, rolled it into the typewriter and punched a few keys. "Seems to be working okay."

I assured him the typewriter was in good condition. I also sweetened the deal with the dollar or so of loose change in my pocket.

"I seen these machines in the pawnshop for twenty dollars," Fred said to the older man. "That tank of his couldn't hold much more than five dollars' worth."

Fred turned toward me and held out his hand. "You got a deal, Mr. Businessman. I'll cover that tank of gas for you."

He put on a raincoat and went to the pumps. I listened to the news report on the scratchy radio. The outer bands of Hurricane Betsy with sustained winds of 160 miles per hour had slammed into the lower regions of the Mississippi River Delta with the heavy storm surge devastating all towns along the river south of New Orleans. The hurricane, now a Category 4, was on track to hit just west of New Orleans in the early evening.

"Glad I'm not down there in all that," the older man said. "The wind and rain will be bad enough when it gets up this way."

I walked over to a coffee pot sitting on a hot plate. "C----ould you throw in a c----up of this coffee?"

The man handed me a white mug after wiping out the insides with a shop rag.

"Help yourself. Made it this morning, but I just cut it off."

I drank the lukewarm sludge while the radio news continued.

The hurricane was predicted to be downgraded to a tropical storm on Friday as it continued through the Mid-South and eventually lose its power in the Upper Midwest where fall crops would benefit from the rain.

Fred shook out his raincoat as he came through the door. "Least you won't have them lovebugs to worry with. Ol' Betsy done blowed 'em all away."

I fished in my pocket for coins and offered them to Fred.

"Keep it, Mr. Businessman. Buy you a Coca-Cola and a candy bar on up the road. It's on Fred."

I went over to the typewriter, pulled the fleur-de-lis bandana from my back pocket and wiped it down. I typed four words on the shop ticket: student, servant, seller, seeker.

"It's good to go," I said to Fred.

★ ★ ★

VINCE VAWTER

I pulled away from the pumps but only to the spot near the picnic table where I had stopped four days before. Time to complete the final manifest of my journey.

I figured to be home a little after dark, which was enough time to get a few hours of sleep before my early shift, depending on how long it took me to deal with the problems I had created for myself with my parents.

I would tell my father we needed to talk about some things that would be difficult for both of us, but that the time had come. I would tell my mother that I wanted her to go with me to Coldwater, Mississippi, to find Mam. I wanted Mam to come spend the night in our new house, and maybe then I could be more comfortable living in it. Mam might even like to see how the world's greatest central vacuum worked.

I also was going to figure out a way to tell my parents that I was going to stop lying to them and being a sneak with all my eavesdropping, but that I needed for them to show more confidence in me and let me make more of my own decisions.

At the newspaper, my plan was to gather the copy editors to tell them the story of how Charlie Roker got the name Rocket. That would be our name for Charlie from then on. I would tell the story in the newspaper way and with the voice that was given to me—not the voice I would have chosen, but one that could serve me well if I would only let it.

I was going to see my college advisor on the first day of school and ask to have my class schedule redone so I could take a foreign language as a freshman. First-year French. If I could stutter in English, I could learn to stutter in French just as well.

I pulled out my billfold and my two special dollar bills. I read the familiar four words on the old taped-together bill. Now that

232

I was satisfied I had figured what the words meant, I had to get serious about the business of turning them into a life well lived.

On the newer dollar bill in the familiar handwriting, I read:

Look not so much to the destination, Messenger, but always to the journey.

C. Spiro

My manifest assured me I had everything I needed.

Q&A with Vince Vawter

Q: Why did you decide to write _Copyboy_?

A: Even though _Paperboy_ met with a success beyond my dreams, I informed my agent that I would not be writing a sequel. I had told my story exactly how I wanted, and I felt a sequel would only mean more rehashing of that part of my life.

About two and a half years after _Paperboy_ was published, I was speaking at a middle school in Florida where the faculty had arranged for me to have lunch with a few of the students. A student came up to me and asked me what happened to Mr. Spiro. I explained that I could tell her what happened to all the other characters in the book because they were based on real people from my childhood, but I could not tell her about Mr. Spiro because he was fictional. At that moment a tear started rolling down her cheek. She said, "I know that . . . but you made him up once and so you can make him up again."

As soon as I got on the plane heading home, I started outlining the narrative for _Copyboy_.

I also looked back at the hundreds of emails and letters I had gotten from readers who wanted to know if Mam continued to live with my family; did I continue to play baseball when I was older; what exactly did the four words on the dollar bill mean?

I decided I owed my readers answers to those questions. _Copyboy_ attempts to answer those questions and more.

Q: What exactly was a copyboy?

A: In the days before computers, newspapers depended upon people called runners, copy clerks, or copyboys to distribute proofs, strip newswire copy from the Teletype machines, and perform hundreds of small tasks that kept newsrooms operating efficiently. The job was entry level but seen as a good way to break into the newspaper business. The position is all but extinct now.

Q: Why did you skip six years to pick up the story?

A: As I mentioned, I felt to tell more of the eleven-year-old boy's story would be redundant. I decided to let him grow for six years and continue his story at that point. In a sense, I wanted the boy to mature along with his younger readers so they could see his challenges through the eyes of a seventeen-year-old.

Q: You have stated that _Paperboy_ is autobiographical. Is the same true for _Copyboy_?

A: Yes, but to a lesser degree. For instance, I did make a trip from Memphis to New Orleans in my tiny two-seater car when I was seventeen. I did work at a newspaper at an early age. I did live through a hurricane in Louisiana the fall after I got out of high school. I did have friends in South Louisiana who lost their homes to Hurricane Betsy in 1965. I did continue to struggle with my stutter as a young adult.

Q: You use four hyphens (----) to denote a stutter when Victor is speaking. How did you come up with that?

A: I refer to that as a "stuttering icon." The replication of a stutter in print is difficult since no two stutters are ever the same. I use the icon to state simply: "He stutters here."

Q: How do you decide where to place the icons?

A: All I can say is that I feel it.

Q: You have said that you don't like to think of yourself as a writer of "books for young people only." What do you mean by that?

A: I consider myself a teller of stories that all ages can enjoy. I believe readers can absorb my books at different levels and gain something no matter what their ages. After all, how many books for young people deal with the teachings of Friedrich Nietzsche? I first read *The Old Man and the Sea* by Hemingway when I was twelve, and I am much the better for it. I understand that books have to be categorized for the marketplace and for library shelves, but when a writer starts relating a story with a certain age group in mind, there's a tendency to "write down" to the audience. I never want to be guilty of that.

Q: You seem to spend a lot of time in the book tracking the path of Hurricane Betsy. How accurate is your portrayal of the deadly storm?

A: The path and timeline of Hurricane Betsy are precise down to the day and even to the hour. I researched National Oceanic and Atmospheric Administration charts and reports extensively to tell the hurricane's story as accurately as I could.

On Thursday, September 9, 1965, the Category 4 hurricane came ashore near New Orleans in the early evening. More than eighty people died, and damage was tabbed at $1.4 billion, the first hurricane to eclipse the billion-dollar mark. Betsy's storm surge caused massive destruction along the river, prompting the U.S. Corps of Engineers to design and build a complex levee system that was guaranteed to protect New Orleans, the same system that failed forty years later during Hurricane Katrina. The National Weather Service vowed there would never be another hurricane named Betsy.

Q: You also describe in great detail the lower Mississippi River around Venice, Louisiana. How accurate is that portrayal?

A: The description is accurate for 1965, but don't expect to find it that way now. Wetlands equivalent in square miles to the state of Delaware have disappeared from the lower Mississippi River in the past 75 years. Environmentalists estimate a chunk of the Gulf Coast the size of a football field is lost every hour to open water. The reasons for the loss of the protective barrier are many and complicated, but man is to blame for much of the deterioration. Each hurricane or tropical storm becomes more of a threat to the Gulf Coast as more of the lower delta retreats to the sea. I visited Venice and the surrounding area in 2017 after a fifty-year absence. I did not recognize it. Read more at mississippiriverdelta.org.

Vince Vawter was reared in Memphis and spent forty years in the newspaper business as a writer, editor, and publisher. He is the author of *Paperboy*, winner of a 2014 Newbery Honor. He and his wife live on a small farm near Knoxville, Tennessee.

Visit him online at vincevawter.com.